You've connected.

danger.com

@8//Dead Man's Hand/

danger.com

@8//Dead Man's Hand/

by
jordan.cray

Aladdin Paperbacks

VISIT US ON THE WORLD WIDE WEB
www.SimonSaysKids.com/net-scene

First Aladdin Paperbacks edition September 1998

Aladdin Paperbacks
An imprint of Simon & Schuster Children's Publishing Division
1230 Avenue of the Americas
New York, NY 10020

The text of this book was set in 11.5 point Sabon.
Printed and bound in the United States of America
10 9 8 7 6 5 4 3 2 1

Library of Congress Cataloging-in-Publication Data
Cray, Jordan.
Dead man's hand / by Jordan Cray.
— 1st Aladdin Paperbacks ed.
p.   cm. — (Danger.com ; @8)
Summary: While on a brief vacation in Key West, sixteen-year-old Annie and her stepbrother Nick do an internet search that inadvertently involves them in a dangerous murder mystery.
ISBN 0-689-82383-5 (pbk.)
[1. Stepfamilies—Fiction. 2. Mystery and detective stories.] I. Title. II. Series: Cray, Jordan. Danger.com ; @8.
PZ7.C85955De   1998
[Fic]—dc21   98-25238
CIP   AC

//prologue

Most people are unhappy most of the time. Most people aren't satisfied with what they have. Most people, let's face it, hate their jobs. And there're a whole lot of people out there who hate their lives.

So it's funny how they hold on to life, isn't it? Funny how they're all so scared of dying. Everyone is always complaining about being tired, about working too hard. You'd think they'd want a nice, long rest.

So you could say I was doing a service, if you look at it that way. I'm giving them the longest rest of all.

Okay. Now you're thinking I'm trying to

justify myself. I'm always going to be one step ahead of you, so don't bother trying to out-guess me.

This isn't justification. This is truth.

I got started in this whole thing for the best of reasons. I had the greater good in mind, okay? The money was not a consideration. Until I started thinking about it.

You want to tell me money isn't important? You want to blame me for grabbing my slice of the pie?

Go ahead. I won't be able to hear a word. I'll be lying on a beach in Bora Bora, listening to the waves.

One step ahead of you? Ha! Try a million miles. Because I've learned an important thing. Once you've thought the unthinkable, the unthinkable becomes thinkable. Even doable. Everyone says, *Just do it!*

So I did.

you've got mail!

To: sohopunk@cyberspace.com
(Nick Annunciato)
From: outRAGme@cyberspace.com
(Annie Hanley)
Re: you gotta be kidding

Homework? HOMEWORK? Do you expect me to buy that excuse, buster? Talk about lame.

Last weekend it was a bad cold. Before that, the snowstorm—the ferry wouldn't be running, you said. Like you're an expert on my ferry. Guess what—the ferry ran all weekend. No disruption in schedule. Quel surprise, n'est-ce pas? You see how bored I am? I have time to study French.

Nick, you are my very first almost-sorta-stepbrother, and you're letting me down, big time. You haven't visited us for three whole months. You can tell me, bro. Is it my breath?

This is Scull Island, fella. It's been a lo-ong winter. I am going out of my stark staring mind. And your dad is seriously missing you.

What gives, hotshot?

```
To: outRAGme@cyberspace.com
From: sohopunk@cyberspace.com
Re: you're right . . .
```

. . . it IS your breath. must be all that garlic my dad cooks with.

just kidding, annie. you called me on it. the big homework excuse was lame, I admit. things are hectic here. maybe a little crazy. but not to worry, because basically, they're great.

i'll download on you when i see you. did dad tell you about key west yet? he's got some food gig down there, all expenses paid, and for some insane reason, he wants the family along. lucky for us it's during spring break. you know how dad is about *our making those children-of-divorce con-nections.*

To: sohopunk@cyberspace.com

From: outRAGme@cyberspace.com

Re: reason to live

He told me tonight. Florida! Color me there.

Just when I'm convinced that life has no meaning, I get five whole days in the sun with nothing to do but hang. You'd better not bag on me. Whatever is going on with your hectic, crazy existence, I don't wanna know. I still haven't recovered from our Christmas adventure. Include me out of your wise-guy schemes, city boy. I need a rest.

To: outRAGme@cyberspace.com

From: sohopunk@cyberspace.com

Re: puh-leeze

wimp.

1//some break

On the morning we left for Key West, my stepfather, Joe, poked his head into my room. "Annie, you ready?"

I zipped up my suitcase. "I've been ready my whole *life* for this. Get me off this island of the dead before I implode!"

Joe grinned. Even though he'd showered and dressed, he still looked rumpled. My stepfather always looks as though he's unraveling. Maybe it's because he doesn't feel comfortable tucked in, or with shoes on. Even on his wedding day, he'd spent half the reception in his socks.

"I know how tough it is for you to tear yourself away from Scull Island," he said.

Don't get me wrong. I love where I live. Scull Island is this tiny place stuck out in Long Island Sound. There's no bridge to the mainland, so we're pretty isolated. All this can be great about half the year. The beaches are uncrowded, and you can hike and swim and eat an ice-cream cone without 60 million people rubbing their suntan oil against you and yelling, *Yo, Pete! Whaddya want on your hot dog?*

But in the winter, we kids call it Dull Island. The year-round population shrinks to ten people. Well, okay—maybe not ten. Maybe about three hundred. But the island feels desolate, and wind comes off the water like a frigid Arctic blast, and everyone just wants to stay inside their house, inhaling central heating. I spent one entire weekend in February perfecting my Nerf basketball hook shot. No lie.

Which is why I was totally bummed that Nick had bagged weekend after weekend. Nick's electric presence can jazz up even Scull Island.

I call Nick my "sort-of stepbrother." He's Joe's son, but we've never lived in the same house. Nick lives in Manhattan with his mom, who is this incredibly busy assistant district attorney. We're more like friends than steps. We're both the same age, six-teen-and-a-half.

Joe and my mom just got married last summer, and Nick visited us at Christmas. We had a major adventure, but it's a long story, and I don't want to pull a Grandad Gus. Grandad Gus is my mom's father. He'll start to tell you something easy, like how to get to downtown Hartford, and he'll wind up telling you this long story about what happened to him in 1956. Not that the story isn't interesting, but you're really more interested in directions.

Are you still with me? If you haven't wandered off to turn on the TV, let me return to my conversation with Joe.

"I am so out of here!" I said, just as Mom arrived, two suitcases slung across her shoulders.

"Kate! Let me do that!" Joe tried to untangle the straps from Mom's shoulders and nearly made her topple over. Mom started to giggle. Joe turns her into a twelve-year-old, I swear.

She was just a nice, normal mom a year ago. She worked downtown in the real estate office and wrote short stories in her spare time. She tried not to say bad things about my dad, who lives in Montana and makes about a million dollars buying up ranch land and selling it to movie stars. She cried at romantic comedies and laughed at my jokes. She cooked things like hamburgers and meat loaf for dinner. Then she went out on a blind date with an Italian chef. The very next day, she threw our green can of processed Parmesan cheese in the garbage and grated a huge hunk of cheese that smelled like vomit on our spaghetti. I knew I was in trouble.

You may suspect that I am not the easiest person in the world to please. So it was a complete surprise to me that about five minutes after Joe Annunciato walked into our front door the very first time, I just about fell for him, too.

"If we make it to the ferry on time, it will be a miracle," Mom said as she dropped the suitcases on the floor with a thump. "Did we lock the garage and toss out the rest of the milk and turn off the hot water heater

. . . what am I missing . . . oh, water the plants?"

"Check," Joe said.

"We'd better hurry. If we miss the ferry, we miss the plane," Mom fretted. "I should double-check the stove." She hurried away. "Annie, make sure you unplugged your hair dryer!"

At the Hanley-Annunciato abode, leaving is chaos. Joe is never ready, Mom thinks the house will blow up if we don't unplug every appliance, and I usually pack my entire wardrobe and forget essential things like underwear.

Somehow, we made it to the ferry on time. Joe pulled the car into a spot, and we all headed up on deck. Even though it was April, there was still snow on the ground on the island. The wind was fierce and made our eyes tear.

"In a few hours, we'll be in eighty-degree weather," Joe said, slipping an arm around each of us.

"Hard to believe," Mom said. "I hope I didn't forget anything."

"Oh, my gosh!" I cried.

"What?" Mom asked, panicked.

"We forgot to feed the dog!"

"Oh, my gosh!" Mom shrieked. Then, she squinted at me. "Hey. We don't have a dog."

The ferry horn blasted, destroying our hearing for the next two minutes. The ferry slowly reversed out of the slip and chugged into open sea.

We watched Scull Island recede into the distance.

Mom sighed. "There it goes. Now we'll have five days of sunshine and nothing to do. Don't be too sad, Annie," she teased.

"I am so totally crushed," I said.

Nick was waiting at the gate, dressed in black jeans and a black sweater. His only luggage was a black leather backpack. His laptop was tucked under his arm. My sort-of step is never difficult to spot. Just look for your average cat burglar.

"I see you're dressed for the tropics," I said as we walked up.

"I don't adapt well," Nick said. He kissed my mom, hugged Joe, and then hugged me. One good thing about Nick is that he's never too cool to demonstrate affection.

We went through the usual boarding hassle. We couldn't get seats all together, so Nick and I took the two seats in the front, and Joe and Mom took seats in the back so Mom could be near the bathroom. She's got a thing about being near the bathroom on planes.

Then we waited with a horde of people until they called out our rows, after which we stood in line with a horde of people and shuffled onto the plane, where we stood packed in the aisle for ten minutes while people hauled huge bags full of crud into the overhead bins, which would probably pop open during turbulence and conk us on our heads.

"Gosh, vacations are fun," Nick said.

But finally, the plane lifted off, and we banked over beautiful downtown Hartford. In a few minutes we were above the clouds, and were promised "premium breakfast service." It turned out to be a defrosted mini-bagel and a miniature package of cream cheese.

Nick and I ordered sodas, since Mom and Joe couldn't see us from where we were sitting. Everyone around us was drinking orange juice and coffee, and we clinked our little plastic glasses of carbonated caramelized sugar together.

"Bon voyage," Nick said.

"Isn't somebody supposed to say that to us?" I asked.

He shrugged. "Who knows? You're the French expert."

I settled back into my seat. "So, spill. I am waiting to hear why you completely abandoned me this winter. And it better be excellent."

Nick sighed.

I nudged him with my shoulder. "Did your mother ground you because you hooked up free cable again? Try to hack into the CIA? Scalp her Knicks tickets? C'mon. You can tell me."

"Oh, Annie," Nick said. "I'm in love."

My mouth dropped. It was lucky there was no bagel and cream cheese in it. Then I realized he must be kidding. Nick was too way past cool to fall in love. "Don't tell me," I said. "You've fallen for Leonardo DiCaprio, too."

"Annie, I'm serious," Nick said. "This is it." His eyes were glassy, as though he were airsick. Uh-oh. I've been there. I recognize the signs of love. They're awful.

"Don't worry, Nick," I said urgently. "I'll get you through it, bro. We'll cruise babes in the Keys, hang out, swim . . . in five days, you won't even remember her name."

"Pia Larkworthy." Nick said the name as though it were a poem. It sort of was, actually. "It's okay, Annie. For some insane reason, she loves me, too."

"Oh." I had assumed Nick's grand passion was unrequited. In the Annie Hanley universe, all true love was unrequited.

It isn't that Nick isn't prime boyfriend material. He has a big nose, like Joe, but it fits into his face okay. He has thick dark hair and big brown eyes. And even though he's a C-breaking student, he's incredibly smart. I just didn't expect another girl to get him the way I do.

"She's amazing. Incredible. She's got this way of wearing a T-shirt, or, like, doing her hair, that's totally radical," Nick burbled. "Plus, she's, like, really talented. She plays the violin. But she *rocks* on that thing. She's awesome."

"I can see that she's turned you into a Valley Girl," I said. "Now *that's* talent."

"We met downtown, in Washington Square Park, but Pia's family has megabucks. She lives on the Upper East Side, and her father works in publishing. He's this incredible intellectual. Her mother is a writer. And Pia is—"

"Really dumb?"

"Brilliant. Plus she's incredibly together for her age. She says she's really intuitive, but she doesn't let that scare her. She goes with it."

"She sounds . . ." *Nauseating. Awful. Unbearable. Insufferable.* " . . . neat," I said.

"She's perfect," Nick said. He leaned over and dug in his backpack. He came up with a bundle of letters tied with a piece of red silk yarn.

"We've written each other a letter for each day we're apart. We're going to read one letter at twelve noon every day. Pia says we'll be spiritually close."

"Whew," I said. "That's really good,

because I was worried about your spiritual growth."

Nick just nodded happily. He didn't even catch *sarcasm* anymore. He was totally gone.

Where did my sort-of stepbrother go? The last time I'd seen him, he was too cool to commit. Every single girl on Scull Island had practically thrown herself in front of him, grabbed his ankles, and begged for his attention. Nick had only paid attention to me.

Color me shallow. I missed that. Now, Nick's eyes were glazed over, and he was staring out at a puffy white cloud as if it were the most fascinating thing in existence. In the absence of Pia, that is.

Then, Nick wrenched his gaze back to me. "I guess I'm obsessing, aren't I?" he said, sounding like the real Nick.

"A tad," I admitted.

He half-turned to face me. "Okay. Enough about Pia. Tell me about you. What do *you* think of Pia?"

He was only joking, thank goodness, so I laughed.

"What's going on?" Nick continued. "Is

Pepper Oneida still the most obnoxious giggle-girl on the planet? Has Josh Do-nothing caught on to her yet?"

"Josh Doolittle," I corrected happily. Josh is my ex-boyfriend. Pepper had snagged him in a disgusting display of eyelashes and midriff-baring baby T-shirts. They were Enemy Numbers One and Two on Nick's and my Hit List. "He's still totally snagged," I added. "But last week, they had this major fight in the cafeteria—"

"Really? Pia and I haven't had one fight," Nick said. "I find that amazing, but Pia says it's because our minds are congruent."

"That's funny," I said. "Because to me, you're such a parallelogram, and she seems so . . . trapezoidal."

But I guess Nick didn't get geometry references. I think I mentioned that he isn't such a great student. "It's incredible, because Pia is so sharp, you know?" he said. "But also amazingly sweet."

Who was this guy? He was using words like "amazing" and "incredible" practically in every sentence. That's what love will do to you. Which only confirms my belief that love is the most awful calamity that could befall a person.

"Anyway, my best friend, Rochelle, heard the whole thing," I continued, still trying to communicate with the love-zombie at my side. "She said that Josh—"

"It's twelve o'clock," Nick interrupted.

"Yeah," I said. "Thanks for the time check. Anyway, Rochelle—"

But he was already unwinding the ribbon from his stack of papers. "I have to read Pia's first letter!"

Nick began to read with this sickly sweet smile on his face, like he'd just stuffed his mouth with Double-Stuf Oreos.

"Where are you going?" he asked, his eyes glued to the paper.

"To borrow a barf bag," I said.

"Mmmm," Nick said. "Good luck."

I sighed as I headed back to say hello to Joe and Mom. Even though they could get gooney since they were technically honeymooners, they still shared at least one functioning brain between them.

Only three months before, Nick was my

partner in crime. He'd had guts and brains and a devilishly scheming mind. Together, we had solved the Three Fat Brothers Pizza Murder. We'd gone toe-to-toe with a madman who'd tried to kill us.

Now the guy who'd saved my life, whose mind had totally clicked with mine, had turned into a drooling sap. This was turning out to be some spring break!

2//too many cooks

The thump of the landing gear woke me up from my nap. We were landing in Miami.

"Wake up, sleepyhead," Nick said. "You've been snoozing since North Carolina."

I yawned. "Sorry. Did I miss a chapter in the riveting Pia-and-Nick saga?"

This time, Nick got the dig. He gave me a sidelong look.

"Or were you too busy being congruently spiritual with her imaginary person?" I inquired.

"I thought you'd be happy for me," Nick said.

"I'd turn cartwheels, but we're landing," I said.

The plane bumped down on the runway. Everyone in the plane gave that collective sigh of relief that we didn't crash.

"I should have known," Nick said, shaking his head. "You're jealous. That whole thing with Josh, first of all. But Pia really called it."

"Pia called what?" I asked.

"She said you had me all to yourself. A new brother and all. And that you might have trouble processing my relationship."

I felt my blood pressure rise to the danger level. "I don't have trouble processing," I said sweetly. "I have trouble keeping my food down when I see that your brain has turned into a mush melon!"

Nick grabbed his backpack from under the seat. He stood up. "Great. Thanks for your support, Annie."

"Don't mention it," I snarled.

But then we had to stand there for fifteen minutes until the plane door opened and everybody grabbed bulging bags from the overhead compartments. It was sort of anti-climactic, let me tell you. After that exchange, at least one of us should have stalked off.

Nick was probably as relieved as I was

when we rejoined Mom and Joe. We all trudged through about a million miles of corridors to get to the charter airline that the Cuisine Channel had booked for our flight to Key West.

Nick looked out the window at the small plane. "We're flying on *that?*"

"Should be a beautiful flight," Joe said.

"It's so . . . *small,*" Nick said.

"Too bad Pia isn't here to hold your yiddle hand," I said. Okay, I was pushing the envelope. But how could I resist?

Nick ignored me. I can't say I didn't deserve it. I slumped in my chair and watched the other passengers arrive.

"Buon giorno!" a stocky man in jeans and a faded green polo shirt called to no one in particular. He dropped his suitcase on the floor with a crash. "Heading down to the Key Lime Food Festival?"

Joe introduced himself and Mom, then said, "And these are our kids, Nick and Annie."

"Glad to meet you," the man said. "I'm the Mediterranean Maestro."

Joe looked at him blankly.

"Bob Summerhall," the man added. "Call me Bob. Guess you haven't heard of me . . . yet. You've heard of *Ben Cotto* magazine, right?"

Joe shook his head. "Sorry."

"I write a food column for them. Travel around the Mediterranean, mostly around Morocco and such. I just spent a winter in Tunisia. Incredible place." Bob still looked cheerful, even though Joe hadn't heard of him.

A woman walked up, dragging her suitcase on wheels. "Is this the plane to Key West?" She had blond hair worn in tight curls and was wearing sunglasses.

"Sure is," Bob said.

"Whew. I think I must have walked ten miles." She dropped into a seat.

"Mediterranean Maestro," Bob said, sticking out his hand. "Bob Summerhall."

"Marcia Fallows," the woman said. "Food critic."

"I think we've met," Joe said. "I'm Joe Annunciato—"

"Of course," Marcia said.

"I think we're neighbors," Joe said.

"Don't you have a place on Scull Island? I've seen you in town."

"Small world," Marcia said. "I took a place for weekends. Escaping the rat race. You know." She checked her watch. "Shouldn't we be boarding?"

If she was escaping the rat race, Marcia Fallows sure looked tense. Even her hair looked nervous.

Behind Marcia, a tall man with prematurely gray hair quietly took a seat. He looked at the plane, looked at his watch, and opened a magazine.

Just then a woman in a blue shirt and khaki pants arrived at the desk. "Sorry for the delay, folks," she said. "We had some thunderstorm activity in the Lower Keys. But we're cleared to fly, so if you'll check in with me, we'll get you boarded and on your way."

"At last," Marcia Fallows said, standing up.

We went through a door onto the tarmac, then climbed the gangway into the small plane. Nick looked uneasy as he strapped into a seat. The khaki-clad attendant leaned over him. "Don't worry. I've flown this plane on this route thousands of times."

"You're the pilot?" Nick squeaked.

She nodded. "Just call me Crash Kazinsky."

Nick turned white.

"That's a joke, hon," she said, patting his shoulder. I burst out laughing, and she winked at me before walking away.

"What a card," Nick said sourly. "Already, I love Florida."

Just then a large, blond man appeared in the doorway. "Howdy, folks!" he boomed in a southern accent. "Hope you didn't hold the plane for little ol' me! My connection was late—I had a book signing in Minneapolis. Those poor folks waited in the snow, just to meet me. Brrrrr." He scanned the passengers. "Parks! You old silver-tailed fox, you! I didn't know *you'd* be attending this soiree."

"It was last minute, Chip," the tall, quiet man replied. "I'm glad to see you, too."

There was a tinge of irony in the man's voice. I looked at Chip, but he ignored the silver-haired man.

"Chip, I'm Marcia Fallows. From

Foodstuff magazine?" Marcia said. "I'm doing an article on you."

"I'm pleased to meet you, young lady," Chip said, leaning over and shaking Marcia's hand vigorously. He squeezed into the seat next to her and looked across the aisle at Joe. "Now, I know you." He glanced at Bob Summerhall. "But I don't know you."

Quick introductions were made all around. It was like being at a party, except we were in a sardine can that was about to take off.

Apparently, Chip was a major hotshot on the Cuisine Channel. For a chef, he acted like a movie star.

"Chip Waddell," Joe whispered to us as the plane taxied down the runway. "He's got the number one show *and* the number one cookbook in the country—they're both called *Hot Stuff*. He and Parks McKenna used to be partners. They owned a restaurant together, but it went under."

We lifted into the air. Nick closed his eyes as we banked over Miami. I could see sweat on his forehead. You had to feel sorry for the guy.

"Want my barf bag?" I asked.

Nick gave me a nasty look. What can I say? Try to be helpful, and look what happens.

By the time we arrived at the hotel, Nick had recovered from his plane-fright. Joe had booked us at an incredible inn. Nick and I had adjoining rooms and shared a porch. There were two pools on the property, and you could rent bicycles.

"Last one in the pool is a scaredy-cat city boy!" I called as I hightailed it to my room.

I changed into my suit in about two minutes flat, but Nick still beat me downstairs. He was already floating on his back, his eyes closed. His skin looked tan against his bathing suit. Meanwhile, I looked as if I'd been dunked in a bucket of milk. I inherited my red hair and freckles from my mom. It is seriously hard for me to tan, but I was going to give it my best shot.

I jumped in, giving him a hefty splash. "Can you believe how hot it is here? It was thirty degrees this morning in Connecticut. It's like we're in a whole other country."

"It ees called par-a-dise," Nick said in a funny accent.

"So what do you want to do before dinner?" I asked. "Joe has to check in at the Food Festival. We could explore Duval Street."

"Actually," Nick said, "I have a mission."

I leaned against the side of the pool and kicked my legs lazily. "Prepare to share."

Nick stroked closer. "It's about Pia, so don't go ballistic on me."

What a surprise. But I felt a little guilty about my behavior on the plane, so I plastered a smile on my face and said, "Go ahead. I'm interested . . . really."

"Well, I have to admit I have a parental problem." Nick hooked an arm around the ladder. "It's her dad. He's not crazy about me, to tell you the truth. He's got some Ivy League–bound hotshot in mind for his darling daughter. So I figure I've got to soften him up."

"Good idea," I said. "What's your plan?"

"He's a cigar fiend," Nick said. "I'm

going to buy him a box of Cubans while I'm here."

"Hold the phone," I said. "Aren't Cuban cigars illegal?"

"Yeah," Nick said. "What's your point?"

"You can't just stroll into a store and buy them, for one," I said. "How are you going to find them?"

"Where you find any contraband," Nick said. "On the Web. I'm already trolling for sites. There's got to be someone here in Key West who sells them. We're practically in Havana's backyard."

"I guess," I said dubiously. "But you'd be dealing with a criminal."

"Again, what's your point?" Nick said, grinning. "You'll come with me to buy them, won't you?"

"Me?" I squeaked. "Why do you need me?"

"Come on, Annie. You're my partner in crime," Nick wheedled. "It will be an adventure. Something to impress your friends with when you get back."

Under normal circumstances, Nick could probably talk me into his plan. Under normal circumstances, Nick could talk me into anything. But I was supposed to help him find contraband in a strange town in order to help him with Pia? I don't think so!

"Sorry, bro," I said, swimming away. "You're on your own."

Nick made a clucking noise, like a chicken.

I ducked under the water. When I shot to the surface, he clucked again.

"Excuse me?" I said. "Who was the sweaty guy with the white knuckles on the plane an hour ago?"

Nick made the chicken noise again. I swam to the ladder and got out of the pool. I ignored him as I settled into a chaise.

"*B-roooark, brrooark brooark . . .*" Nick clucked.

The next time I go on a family vacation, do me a favor. Remind me to leave my family home, will you?

3//mile zero

You can't find yourself in paradise without cheering up. Key West is stuck out in the middle of an aquamarine sea. It has quirky old houses and bushes that bloom with red and pink and purple flowers. Every night, there was a party at the wharf to celebrate the sunset, as though it were some incredible occurrence. In Key West, it is.

All the next day, the family rented bicycles and bi-wheeled around. We visited Ernest Hemingway's house and petted his six-toed cats. We ate stone crab claws and key lime pie. We bought the silliest T-shirts we could find.

Everywhere we went, Nick bought a present for Pia. A key chain, a sweatshirt, a mug from this restaurant called Margaritaville. It was truly sickening.

Soon, the complimentary duffel Joe got from the Food Festival was stuffed with presents for Pia.

Nick didn't have much luck trolling the Net, so he finally left a posting on the Food Festival Web site. It was my suggestion. I figured that the festival attracted major foodies, and some of them probably loved cigars, so why not? Cigars are trendy, and the food festival was full of trendoid types.

from: sohopunk
I'm in Key West looking for the obvious contraband. Anybody out there have access to some muy bueno smokes?

Nick didn't think it would be too cool to use the word "Cuban" in the posting. We figured the Spanish would be a good clue.

The next morning, Nick knocked at my door before breakfast. I stumbled my way to the door.

"Somebody answered my posting!" he told me.

I yawned. "Awesome."

"His online name is Imp.Exp," Nick said. "He's got Cubans. Expensive, though."

"How much?" I asked.

"We agreed on two hundred for a box," Nick said, wincing.

"You're spending *two hundred dollars* on Pia's father?" I was awake now. "Are you insane?"

"If it will buy me a summer of hassle-free contact with Pia, it's worth it," Nick swore.

I sighed. "When are you meeting this bozo?"

"Tonight," he said. "The timing is perfect. Dad and Kate are going out for dinner. We're supposed to eat in the inn. It would be no problem to go for a quick walk. "Now, are you going to help me or not?"

I headed to the bathroom and splashed water on my face. I felt more awake, which helped me to realize clearly that what I was about to do was bone-stupid. I looked at my dripping face in the mirror and slicked back my hair.

Don't be stupid, Annie. You haven't been in trouble with your parents all winter. This has hands-off written all over it.

"Okay, I'll do it," I told Nick.

"I knew you wouldn't let me down," Nick said.

"Your brain is so love-fried, you need protection," I said.

Hand in hand, Joe and Mom took off to eat Italian food at Antonia's.

"Stay close to the inn," Joe told us.

"Be back by dark, okay?" Mom said.

"We promise," Nick and I chorused.

As soon as they vanished from sight around the corner, Nick turned to me. "We have time to grab some dinner," he said.

"What time are we meeting the guy?" I asked.

"Ten o'clock."

"Ten? That's cutting it awfully close," I said. "What if Joe and Mom come home by then?"

Nick shook his head. "No way. It's their big night out. They'll eat about five courses, and Joe will have a double espresso, and your mom won't be able to choose, so she'll order two desserts. . . . "

He was right. "But still," I said. "I don't want to get caught."

"It will only take, like, fifteen minutes," Nick promised. "The meeting place is only four blocks away. It's cake."

"Where is it?" I asked suspiciously. "It had better not be someplace dark and isolated. I don't want to break any more rules than I have to."

Nick slung his arm around my shoulders. "No problem, Annie. It's not isolated. We're meeting him in a bar."

4//blue iguana

When you're breaking the rules, there comes a point that you figure, what's one more? Joe and Mom would lock us in our rooms for the remainder of our stay in Key West if they knew we went to a bar. It was a major parental no-no. But then again, buying contraband Cuban cigars from a stranger probably wouldn't rate us a pat on the head, either.

We decided it would be stupid to try to look old enough to be in a bar. If I put on makeup, or Nick smoked a cigarette, we'd just look like two sixteen-year-olds trying to look older. So we hoped the bar would be dark and crowded, and no one would notice us.

We lucked out. The Blue Iguana turned out to be the rip-roaringest place in town.

We could hear the noise from a block away. The bar was painted in cheerful, tropical blues and greens, but the paint had faded and blistered. Oil lanterns were strung along the ceiling and on the tables, and they didn't throw much light. The bar had a rough plank-wood floor and was open on three sides to the warm breezes. It was packed with people of all ages, from their twenties to their seventies, all of them perched on stools or dancing to the juke-box, or drinking margaritas, or waving frosty bottles of beer in friendly arguments.

We were able to slip inside and make our way through the crowd without anyone stopping us.

Nick put his mouth close to my ear. "As long as we don't try to order a drink, we're probably okay," he whispered.

"What does the guy look like?" I asked.

"He said he'd be wearing a shirt with red parrots on it," Nick told me.

We circulated through the bar, but we didn't see anyone in a red-parrot shirt. Frustrated, Nick tried the men's room. Nothing.

I looked at my watch. "We'd better get back, Nick. It's almost ten-fifteen."

"Let's make the rounds one more time," Nick said.

This time, we spotted him. He was in a dark corner, but the red parrots stood out. He had a straw hat pulled low over his forehead. His skinny forearms were tan, with reddish-blond hairs. A tuft of reddish-blond hair stuck out of the top of his shirt. He had a half-empty bottle of Mexican beer in front of him. He rubbed long fingers with bony knuckles up and down the bottle. His left hand rested on a cigar box. A wedding ring glinted in the faint light.

"He looks like a totally shady character," I whispered to Nick.

"What did you expect, a priest? Come on." Nick grabbed my arm and led me over to the dark table. We sat down opposite the stranger.

He looked up, and I caught a flash of blue eyes under the brim of his hat.

"Can I help you?" he asked.

"I think so," Nick said. He slid an envelope across the table. The man didn't touch it. "Two hundred. Just like you said."

The man just stared down at the envelope.

"I'm sohopunk," Nick said impatiently. "We have a deal, right?"

"Aren't you a little young for this business, kid?" The man slowly raised his head. His blue eyes were amused.

"They're not for me," Nick said. "What do you care, anyway?"

The man's puzzled light eyes fixed on me. "What about her?"

"What about her?" Nick said impatiently. "She's my sister. So what?"

"Listen, kid—" the man began.

Nick's chin stuck out belligerently. "You got a problem? We made a deal."

Uh-oh. Nick's temper was flaring. I should have told the guy not to call him "kid."

"Go home," the man said softly. "I think I made a mistake. I think you did, too."

Nick pushed the envelope closer. "We had a deal!"

"Sorry," the man said, tilting his hat brim back down. "No deal. Run home to Mommy."

Nick's face flushed an angry red. I tugged at his sleeve. "Come on, Nick. Let's go back to the inn."

Nick's hand shot out. He pushed the envelope into the man's lap. Surprised, the man reached for it. Nick grabbed the cigar box and tucked it under his arm. "A deal's a deal," he said. Then he yanked me toward the door.

I heard the chair scrape as the man got up to follow us. I heard the tinkle of glass as he knocked over his beer. But I couldn't turn. Nick pulled me along, and we slithered through the packed crowd. At the last minute, Nick reversed direction and pushed through the double doors of the kitchen.

We ran past the startled cooks and busboys and slammed out the rear door. We found ourselves in a dirt parking lot.

"Hurry," Nick grunted.

We ran off underneath the drooping branches of a huge tree with these gnarled, spreading roots. I stumbled over them, but Nick yanked me up again. We ran down an alley, up another street, and hit Duval Street, the main drag.

We melted into the crowd. When we got to the corner, we turned. I caught a glimpse of a straw hat just turning down Duval.

"Hurry, Annie," Nick urged.

We ran down the dark street, breathing hard now. Our footsteps pounded on the sidewalk. We didn't stop until we got to the inn.

We slowed to a walk when we reached it. We paused in the shadow of a huge live oak. We both bent over double, trying to catch our breath.

"See what I mean?" Nick panted. "Cake."

I held my side, which was aching from the run. "At least you got the cigars."

Nick shook the box happily. Then, he held it up against the light. "Annie," he said in a strange voice, "what does that say?"

I peered at the box. "Tampa, Florida."

"That's not in Cuba, is it?"

"No," I said. "The last time I checked, Florida was part of the U.S."

Nick's expression was stunned. "The guy cheated me!"

Just then we heard a rumble of laughter

from the front porch. After our experience, we jumped about a mile in the air.

Parks McKenna stood up from a wicker armchair in a shadowy corner. The light glinted on his silver hair. "Sorry, kids," he said. "I didn't mean to eavesdrop. Sounds like you got taken."

Nick held up the cigar box. "He said they were Cuban."

"How much?" Parks asked.

"Two hundred," Nick said in a disgusted voice.

He laughed. "Sorry, Nick. Didn't mean to laugh. It's just that we all get taken in life. You've learned your lesson early. At least it was a stranger. Some of us get taken by the people we know best."

Parks's gaze became unfocused, as though he already had begun to think of something else. He started toward the front door, but Nick stopped him.

"Mr. McKenna? Um, if my dad—"

He waved behind him without turning. "Don't worry. I won't tell your parents."

You could tell that he wouldn't tell our parents because he didn't care very much and was already bored with our story. But that was fine with us.

We trudged into the lobby and made a beeline for our rooms. Nick opened his door, and we slipped inside.

"Mr. McKenna's right," I said. "You learned a lesson. Could have been worse, I guess." I flopped into an armchair. "I'm just glad it's over."

Nick's face flushed. "It's not over, Annie. We're going back there. Tonight!"

5//smokes

"No way," I said. "It's ten-forty! Mom and Joe will be back any second!"

"I'm not going to let that guy cheat me!" Nick exclaimed.

"Besides, the inn closes its doors at eleven P.M.," I reminded him. "If you're going to be out later than that, you have to ask for a key. And if we ask for a key, you can bet Joe and Mom will find out somehow."

"We can sneak out the window," Nick said.

"We're on the second floor." I shook my head. "I'm not risking my neck for some cigars. Besides, the guy is probably long gone. He thought he could cheat some *turista*, and he did."

"Yeah," Nick said sourly. "Me. If you hadn't been yanking on my arm, I would have looked at the box."

"Yeah, it's all my fault," I said, waving a hand. "I'm the one who contacts some anonymous person on the Net, goes to a rowdy bar, and hands over two hundred of my very own dollars to a complete stranger."

Nick collapsed on the bed. "Okay, okay. I'm the bozo."

"Besides," I pointed out, "it's not like he gave you the cigars. You *grabbed* them."

"He was going to sell them to me!" Nick protested. "He didn't because I'm underage. Now I'm out two hundred bucks and I have no leverage with Pia's old man."

"Nick, I think it's time for you to let go of the past," I said in a deliberately calm, professional voice. "You have to move on with your life. Don't torture yourself with regrets. Life is short. Then you die. This is the first day of the rest of your—"

There was a soft knock at Nick's door.

"Are you awake?" Joe asked in a whisper.

Nick quickly shoved the cigar box under his bed and opened the door. "We're still up. How was dinner?"

"Sublime," Joe said happily as he came

through the door. "I think I just might have found a place that cooks as good as me. Kate was exhausted, so she went to bed. But I thought I should find out what plans you guys have for tomorrow night. I'm doing that cooking demonstration. There're a couple of seats available." Joe's face creased in a grin. "Well, more than a couple. Chip Waddell is doing his cooking show at the same time, so my demo is not exactly high priority. Do you two want to come?"

Before I could say anything, Nick spoke up. "Gosh, Dad, that sounds great. Really great. But we're here in Key West on vacation, and, no offense, but—"

"You can walk into the kitchen at home and see me cook anytime you want," Joe finished.

"And it is some fun experience, let me tell you," Nick said.

"Don't lay it on too thick, son, I just ate," Joe said. "Okay, I'm hitting the sack." He started toward the door, but he paused with his hand on the knob. "How was your evening?"

"Great!" Nick and I chorused.

"Dinner was good?"

"Great dinner," we said.

"Did you go for a walk, see the sunset?"

We both nodded. "It was great," I said.

Joe paused. "Why do I feel I'm not getting the full story?" He opened the door. "I don't want to know. Good night, kids."

As soon as the door shut behind Joe, Nick turned to me. "Let's go," he said.

"Go where?"

He crossed to the French doors. "We can climb down that porch column," he said. "I think I can swing out to that tree branch—"

"Have a ball, Tarzan," I said with a yawn. I headed for the door. "Wake me up when it's over."

Sometime in the middle of the night, I woke up. I didn't know if it was a dream, or if I'd heard a noise. Maybe a branch had scraped against the window. I peered out at the unfamiliar shadowy shapes in the hotel room. Then I glanced at the red illuminated numbers of the bedside clock. Three-ten A.M.

I heard the noise again. I looked over at my door. My doorknob was turning. I wasn't worried. I knew who my middle-of-the-night visitor was. I knew I'd locked the door, too. Joe is a fanatic about hotel security, since he travels often for his job. He always gives us a safety drill that includes locating the fire exits and putting the chain on the door.

The door opened a crack and thudded softly against the chain.

"Forget it, Nick," I called into the darkness. "I'm not going!"

I flopped back on the pillows, turned over, and went back to sleep.

"It wasn't me," Nick said.

"Yeah, right," I said.

Nick stopped dead in the hotel corridor. We were on our way to breakfast. I hadn't eaten much dinner the night before. I'd been too nervous about our excursion. This morning I was hungry, and I didn't have time for Nick's games.

Nick put his hand on my arm and squeezed. "Annie, it wasn't me. Somebody tried to break into my room, too. I thought it was you."

I could tell that he was serious. "What did you do?"

"I yelled out that I'd changed my mind," Nick said. "I told you to go back to sleep."

Joe and Mom came out of their rooms, dressed in shorts and T-shirts. They headed toward us. Mom suddenly frowned as she came closer. The woman has emotional radar, I swear. "What's wrong?" she asked.

Nick and I quickly explained. Joe and Mom nearly had simultaneous heart attacks. They hustled us down to the front desk and asked for the manager.

We told our story again, and the manager soothed Mom and Joe and called the police. He promised increased security. He looked worried, too. "Did you happen to note the time, miss?" he asked me.

"About three A.M.," I said. "Three-ten, to be exact."

"That's funny," Nick said. "Somebody tried to break into my room at four-fifteen. What was he doing for an hour?"

The manager frowned. Then he turned to me. "Did you set your clock ahead? It was daylight savings time last night."

"No," I admitted. "I was too tired, and I forgot."

"I did," Nick said. "That explains it. He went straight from your room to mine."

The manager sighed. "We just don't have these kinds of problems in Key West," he said.

"Well, now you do," Joe said grimly. "It appears that you had a hotel thief on the premises last night."

First we tangle with a smuggler. Then a thief. Remind me of something next time, will you? The next time I take a family vacation, tell me to stay home.

That night, Joe and Mom didn't want to leave us alone. They cornered us in my room.

"We'll be fine," Nick assured them.

"Promise you'll be careful," Mom said anxiously. "When you're in your rooms, keep the chain on."

"Check."

"And don't hang around outside once it gets dark," she continued.

"Check."

"As a matter-of-fact, stay around people," Mom said. "Don't sit out in the garden if there's nobody else there."

"Kate," Joe said gently, "we're dealing with a hotel thief, not a homicidal maniac."

"I know," Mom fretted. "I just want them to be careful, that's all."

"We'll be careful," Nick promised. "Aren't you going to be late?"

Joe looked at his watch. "You're right. Come on, Kate."

Nick grinned and waved as Joe and Mom took off across the lobby. As soon as they were out of sight, he turned to me. "Perfect," he said. "Joe and Kate are out again tonight. Which means—"

"We have a nice evening here watching TV and ordering room service?" I suggested helpfully.

"We go hunting," Nick said.

6//close, but no cigar

The Blue Iguana was just as crowded as the
night before. It was a dark, moonless night,
and earlier it had rained hard for about an
hour. The steady *drip, drip* of the trees
didn't help my nerves.

All day, I had tried a million reasons
for Nick to stay at the hotel. The weather—only it had stopped raining. The danger—what if the guy was angry at Nick?
The major trouble we'd be in if Joe and
Mom found out. Nick didn't care. He
considers himself a street kid, even
though he now lives in a fairly posh building with a doorman in SoHo. He has this
major honor thing going about being
ripped off.

We slipped inside the bar. The jukebox
was blaring, and some guys who looked like

locals were having some kind of contest at the bar. They were all dressed in ratty T-shirts and shorts and clutching bottles of beer. I listened for a minute, and it turned out they were trying to stump each other on poetry.

"Wordsworth!" one of them shouted.

"Coleridge!" another one screamed.

A short, stocky guy grinned. "Gotcha. Shelley."

Key West is a truly strange place.

"Annie, pay attention," Nick whispered. "And stay out of the bartender's sight, will you?"

We crept through the bar. It was so crowded, I couldn't see into the corners. We had to peer around elbows and backs and stand on our tiptoes. And we had to do this without seeming conspicuous, or letting the guy see *us*. You try it sometime.

I was ready to pack it in when I noticed him. He was standing in a short back hallway, right by the rest rooms. He was talking to someone, but I couldn't tell who it was, or even if it was a man or a woman. He was gesturing and he looked angry.

"He's over there," I told Nick in a low tone. "By the rest rooms."

Nick peered over the heads. "I don't see him."

I looked over. The man was gone.

"He was there!" I said.

Nick and I carefully scanned the tables near the rest rooms. They were all taken, but our man was nowhere to be seen.

"Maybe he went in the men's room," I suggested.

"I'll check," Nick said. "Meanwhile, you stay between him and the door."

Nick melted away through the crowd. He went into the men's room, but came out a few seconds later. He looked at me and shrugged.

I joined him. "He must have gone out the back door to the parking lot," I said.

Nick nodded. "Let's go. And try to stay out of sight. I want to surprise him."

Personally, I thought the guy probably had taken off by now, but I didn't say anything. I just hoped he'd disappeared, and we could go back to the hotel and order dessert from room service.

Nick eased open the door to the parking lot. The dim light only illuminated the first row of vehicles. Cars and pickup trucks were parked in the rear of the lot, underneath the shady trees.

"I don't see him," I whispered.

"Maybe he's toward the back," Nick said. "Follow me."

I'd rather turn around and go in the opposite direction, but I followed. We crept around the perimeter of the lot, trying to keep out of the lone streetlight. We tiptoed around the cars until we were in the rear. Nothing.

"You see? He's gone," I said.

"Yeah," Nick said, disappointed. "Maybe we should check the bar again."

We started back across the parking lot. But just then, I caught a flash of something gleaming under the shade of a tree. Maybe someone had dropped money, or jewelry.

"Hang on," I told Nick. I took a few more steps toward the tree. Its roots were huge, splaying over the dirt like big, gnarled fingers.

I hadn't seen jewelry. I'd seen a belt

buckle. On a person. He was lying on the ground.

I let out a gasp. Nick hurried to stand beside me. My arms and legs stopped functioning. The body wasn't moving, either. The guy looked extremely still.

"Is he okay?" Nick said. "Probably drunk, I guess. I—"

He stopped. Both of us realized who it was at the same time.

"It's him!" Nick breathed.

It was definitely our guy. I recognized the reddish-blond hair on the skinny forearms, the long, big-knuckled fingers on his right hand.

A knife with a long, sharp blade lay near his left foot. The edge of the blade looked sticky and wet.

I clutched Nick's arm. "N-Nick, do you see what I see?"

"Yeah," Nick gulped.

My gaze moved up from his left sneaker to the left arm.

I screamed. He was missing a hand.

7//not again

I hid my face in Nick's shoulder. "Someone cut off his *hand*, Nick!" I hissed.

I felt him nod. I saw him swallow. "Uh, what should we do, Annie?" His voice sounded shaky.

Just then, we heard a twig snap nearby. Then the sound of someone crashing through a bush. Toward us. We looked at each other.

"Run?" I suggested.

We ran. And my track coach thinks I lack motivation! I streaked all the way back to Duval Street. We didn't stop running until we reached the police station.

A cop in shorts was sitting at the front desk.

"Body," I gasped.

"Dead," Nick added. "Stabbed."

I pointed to my hand. "G-gone," I stuttered.

The cop raised an eyebrow. "Are we playing charades?"

"He's under a tree," Nick said. "The dead guy."

"And his hand is gone," I said.

He sighed. "I keep telling the tourists this is *not* Margaritaville, okay? No matter what Jimmy Buffett says."

"We're not drunk," Nick said. He was getting his wind back. "We don't drink. We saw a dead body. I swear. Outside the Blue Iguana."

"But you don't drink," the cop said.

"You've got to believe us!" I said. "He's lying on the far side of the parking lot. Underneath that huge tree—"

"Okay, okay," the cop said. We were getting through to him. "We'll check it out. You kids relax."

We didn't relax. We sat down, shaking, while the cop made a call on the radio. It took about two minutes for the other policeman to report back. He'd found the body.

Cop number one started to take us seriously. He introduced himself—Sergeant Andy Frick—and offered us a soda. That was nice of him. Then he called our parents. We could have done without *that*.

Joe and Mom arrived in about three seconds flat. They were panting, too.

"Not again!" Joe said. He clutched his head with both hands. Sometimes, he's just so Italian.

"What were you doing in a bar?" Mom asked. I'd hoped she would have taken at least a half hour before coming up with that particular question.

"We were going for a walk," Nick said. "It was such a great night."

"It wasn't dark yet," I said. "But then I guess it got dark."

"We weren't *in* the bar," Nick said. "I mean, technically."

"Funny," Sergeant Frick said. "Because the bartender said he saw two kids in the bar tonight. When he went to check their IDs, they were gone."

"That *is* funny," Nick said.

Joe gave Nick his take-no-prisoners look.

"Enough, Nick. We're talking murder here. I want the truth. Right now."

Nick looked at his sneakers for a minute. "Okay," he said. "I'll come clean. We were in the bar. For, like, a couple of minutes. But we didn't drink! I promise. It just looked like so much fun. . . ."

I gazed at Nick. He wasn't going to come clean about the cigars. He knew Joe would have a fit. I thought he was wrong, but I had to back him up. "We left right away, practically," I said.

That's when we found him. Dead. Without a hand," I added.

"Do you have to keep bringing that up?" Nick growled.

"I want to hear all of that again. Slowly," Sergeant Frick said.

So we told him again. We left off the part about having met the dead man the night before. Even though there really wasn't much else to say, the police asked us to go over the story again. Then they took a statement. And the whole time, Joe sat there, glowering at us. He sent Mom back to the inn because she looked so exhausted. I guess one neat part of being married is that you can trade off when it comes to horrible situations with your disobedient kids.

Finally, Sergeant Frick said we were free to go. He told us he might have more questions for us tomorrow. The police had no idea who the dead guy was. Nobody in the bar knew him. He wasn't a regular. He'd had no ID, but he'd had a hotel key in his pocket, and it would take a while to track that down.

Another officer gave us a ride back to the hotel in the patrol car, which was seriously swell. Not because the ride was so exciting—Nick and I had been in a patrol car before—but because it put off Joe's lecture for an additional ten minutes.

Back at the hotel, our ears were blistered by the time Joe finished. I don't have to repeat what he said, do I? It covered the basics: truth, honor, safety, stupidity—you get the picture.

We were in the palatial parental doghouse the next morning, too. Then it was Mom's turn. "We have to be able to trust you," she said. "The way that you can trust us. I'm so disappointed in you both."

Oy. When they're just plain furious, you can cope. But when they're disappointed, you feel like throwing yourself on the floor and bawling like a two-year-old.

"Let's stick close to home today," Joe said wearily. "I say we hang out by the pool and relax."

That sounded just fine by me. I still hadn't perfected my tan. As a matter-of-fact, all I'd accomplished was adding to my freckle quotient.

Sergeant Frick showed up while we were having lunch by the pool. He gave us the unappetizing details.

"We still haven't found that left hand. It was almost surgically severed," he said. "It's not that easy to cut off a hand, you know. And let's face it, it could be anywhere. Could have been thrown in the ocean. Sharks will make short work of it." He looked down at my chicken tostada. "Oh, I didn't mean to interrupt your lunch. Enjoy."

"Thanks," I said, poking at it.

Chip Waddell hustled over from the other side of the pool. "Officer! Officer! Now, I'm just about as lucky as a tick on a hound dog. This will save me a trip to see you. My laptop was stolen last night."

"Where?" Sergeant Frick asked.

"At my taping," Chip Waddell said. His sunburned nose was peeling, and his neck was an angry red. "I was busy cooking and entertaining my fans, and it went missing."

"Taping?" Sergeant Frick frowned, confused.

"I'm Chip Waddell," Chip said. He raised his voice and leaned closer. *"Waddell. Hot Stuff."*

"And that should mean something to me, sir?" Sergeant Frick said politely.

"It should mean plenty," Chip said. His booming down-home manner suddenly changed to irritability. His neck grew even redder. "My point is, I'm reporting a robbery of my personal things."

"I got that," Sergeant Frick said dryly. "I'm afraid you'll have to come to the station to make a report."

"I don't have time to sit around, jawing about my problems," Chip said crankily. "I just want 'em solved."

"We do, too," Sergeant Frick said calmly. "That's why you need to file a report."

"I'll be speaking to your superior officer!" Chip said angrily.

"He'll tell you to make out a report, too," Sergeant Frick said calmly.

Chip puffed himself up, as if he were about to say something. Then he just shook his fat finger at Sergeant Frick and hustled off.

Sergeant Frick sighed. "Last night was quite a night," he said, shaking his head and turning back to us. "I assure you folks, Key West has a fairly low crime rate. A little smuggling, a little illegal conch fishing, maybe a few rowdies now and again. Last night was unusual. Hope you folks didn't get scared off."

"Not at all," Joe said. "But we're scheduled to leave early tomorrow morning. Will you need to talk to Annie and Nick again?"

"You're free to go," Sergeant Frick said. "I have your phone number up north."

"Sergeant Frick, why would the killer cut off a hand?" Nick spoke up. "It can't be to remove fingerprints, since they left the other one."

"Unless they were planning to, and we surprised them," I said.

Nick nodded thoughtfully. "Or there could have been a distinguishing birthmark."

Sergeant Frick looked at both of us. "Who are you guys, Holmes and Watson?"

"You have no idea," Joe groaned. He looked at us sternly. "This is one murder you're *not* going to investigate. Got me?"

"Got you," Nick and I said obediently.

Here's a tip for you: When your parents and a police officer are both in the vicinity, strict obedience is your best call.

"Besides, we're leaving tomorrow," Nick said. "What trouble could we possibly get into?"

"Don't get us started," Mom said.

8//outta here

We had promised Mom and Joe that we wouldn't investigate. But we hadn't said anything about *wondering*.

On the plane the next day, we went over the clues. That took about five minutes. You really couldn't say we had a lot to go on.

Nick summed it up. "So, we've got a dead body and we don't know who he is. He's killed for who-knows-what reason by who-knows-who. He's got a missing hand, and we don't know why. And we were either unlucky to stumble on a random murder, or it has to do with smuggling cigars."

"Or smuggling in general," I added.

"The only connection we know for sure is the Food Festival Web site," Nick said. "For some reason, the guy was monitoring it. That means that the murderer could be someone who was at the festival. It could even be someone we met."

I glanced around the plane. Chip Waddell was talking to Marcia Fallows. Bob Summerhall was snoozing. Parks McKenna was sipping coffee and staring out the window. Not one of them looked like a killer.

"Come on, Nick," I said. "Can you imagine any of those people killing a guy and then hacking off his hand? They all look like they'd freak if their steak was cooked medium well instead of rare."

Nick leaned closer. "Look at it this way, Annie. They all have one thing in common. They're all handy with knives."

We landed in Hartford and all trudged to the baggage claim. I kept my crack detective eye on Nick's suspects.

Marcia kept trying to keep all her various carry-on bags on her shoulders. One or another would keep slipping off and crashing to the floor, where Bob Summerhall would trip over it. Chip Waddell was trying to retrieve messages on his cellular phone, only he kept disconnecting himself. Parks

McKenna went down the wrong corridor and got lost.

"Yeah," I said to Nick. "What a bunch of criminal masterminds."

We waited by the baggage carousel and then grabbed our bags as they merry-go-rounded along.

"All set?" Joe asked. He was carrying three suitcases, and Mom just had her little carry-on. Sometimes he's just so macho.

"I haven't seen my duffel yet," Nick said. "It's the freebie from the Food Festival."

"Make sure to check your ticket," Joe advised. "Everybody got a duffel. You could get it mixed up with someone else's."

"Don't worry," I said. "We can spot Nick's. It's the fattest one. It's crammed with presents for Pia Not-worthy."

"Larkworthy," Nick muttered.

"Whatever," I said.

Just then I noticed Parks McKenna heading toward the exit. A stuffed duffel bag was over one shoulder.

"Hey, Nick," I said. "That looks like . . ."

Nick took off after Parks, and I followed.

"Excuse me, Mr. McKenna!" Nick

called, catching up. "I think that's my bag."

Parks looked at the bag. "It is?"

"Look at the tag," Nick said, lifting it. "See?"

"Oh. Then where's mine?" Parks looked around.

"Probably still on the carousel," I said.

"Oh. Sorry, kid. Here you go." Parks handed over the duffel and ambled off.

"Whew," I said. "That was a close one. What would poor Pia have done without a T-shirt from Margaritaville? Probably cried into her pillow every night."

"Annie, will you chill? If I have to hear one more—" Nick started his rant, but Joe came up and asked if we were ready to go, so we got to make it through an entire vacation without having a major fight.

Nick was staying with us through the weekend, since his mother was on a business trip. I wondered how he could bear having to wait an extra two days before he could see Pia, but I decided not to ask. Once in a while, I do try to curb my obnoxious impulses.

Our arms aching, we walked through a

zillion miles of corridors to get to long-term parking. Joe paid the ransom to get the car out of the garage, and we headed toward New London and the Scull Island ferry.

The weather seemed cold after Florida temperatures, even though it was basically a brisk spring day.

"I'm happy to be home," Mom said, sighing as we drove onto the ferry. "Even that ferry snack bar looks good."

"Don't forget your own rule, Mom," I said. "Any food consumed on the open water has no calories."

Mom laughed as she slipped out of the passenger seat. I noticed she'd put on a few pounds. When you live with a chef, the battle of the bulge is more like a constant war. Maybe I shouldn't have mentioned calories.

We all walked upstairs to the main deck. Joe bought some potato chips and sodas at the snack bar, and we braved the chilly wind on the deck as we motored out into the choppy Sound. Mom was right. There is something about heading home that just makes you happy. The murder seemed very far away. I guessed that Nick and I would gradually lose interest in puzzling over it. One day, it would just be one of those warm and fuzzy family vacation "remember when?" memories.

Remember when we went to Boston and walked the Patriot Trail?

Remember when little Billy did the back-stroke for the first time?

Remember when we found that dead body in Key West?

Well, you get the idea. Some families are just weirder than others.

Slowly, Scull Island grew from a tiny smudge on the horizon to a large smudge in the middle of the sea. The ferry horn blasted, alerting us to get into our cars. The boat was packed today. Tourist season was already beginning.

Our car was first in line. We could see the white froth of the waves as the ferry slowed its engines and began the maneuvers that would allow it to slide into the slip.

"Won't be long now," Joe said.

"Should we stop at the grocery store and pick up a few things?" Mom asked.

"I can go later," Joe said. "I think we should just head back. You look tired, sweetheart."

Mom smiled at Joe. "You worry too much."

A car started its engine behind us, even though the DO NOT START ENGINES UNTIL FERRY IS DOCKED sign was clearly visible.

"Probably a tourist," Joe said, sighing.

Suddenly, we all pitched forward as the car behind us hit our bumper.

"What the . . ." Joe said.

Then the car hit our bumper harder. We pitched forward and kept rolling. Behind us, the car engine whined in a high-pitched, strange way. We rolled further toward the edge. The only thing between us and the cold blue Sound was a teensy metal chain.

The ferry workers looked over, startled, as we kept on rolling.

"I can't stop!" Joe shouted. "Everybody out!"

9//close call

The whine of the engine behind us sounded urgent and mean. We were packed so tightly that we could only open our doors a few inches. Joe slid over on his seat to help Mom squeeze out, while she frantically called, "Annie! Nick!" and didn't move.

"Go, go!" Joe shouted. Nick was halfway out his door, and the driver of the car next to us had seen what was happening and tried to help me squeeze out.

Joe managed to push Mom out. The car veered close to the edge and slammed against the link chain.

"Joe!" Mom screamed.

Joe got one arm out, then a leg. The car slammed against the chain again, and it broke. The two front wheels went over.

"Joe!" Mom screamed again. I screamed, too, something wordless and desperate. Nick scrambled across a car hood, trying to get to his father.

Just at the last possible second, Joe popped out of the opening like a cork. He fell onto the ferry deck, just clearing the car. It tipped over the end of the ferry and splashed into the water below. The second car followed, crashing spectacularly into the sea. I had just enough time to notice that the car was empty.

Two hours later, we were still at the Scull Island police station. Chief Plutsky had brought in sandwiches from the diner and had given us all blankets, as though we'd actually fallen in the water.

The Coast Guard had asked questions, and so had Chief Plutsky. An investigator had flown over from New London in a helicopter. You'd think with all those people they'd have some answers. They had zip.

"They keep saying *freak accident,*" Nick complained to me under his breath.

"Well, it *was* freaky," I said.

He lifted an eyebrow. "But was it an accident?"

Suddenly, I was glad that Chief Plutsky had given me a blanket. I clutched it around my shoulders. "Nick, you're scaring me," I said. "What are you saying?"

"I'm saying it seems like too much of a coincidence to me," Nick said. "We stumble on the scene of a murder, right? And the murderer could have been there. He could have seen us. Watched us. Followed us. Or he could have *already known who we were*."

"Hold your horses, pardner," I said. "You're leaping to a whole bunch of conclusions. You can't connect what happened on that ferry to what happened in Key West."

"*We're* the connection," Nick said.

Chief Plutsky ambled over, stirring his coffee. He sat in a chair opposite our group and leaned toward us, the cup between his knees. I could tell that the chief was still fighting his paunch. If you're a police chief on Scull Island, you don't get to do much running around. You mostly have to sit in the station and listen to people complain about things like parking and kids with loud radios.

"Sorry to keep you folks so long. We're still waiting for details. We don't know who was driving, but we figure the accelerator got stuck. How and why, we don't know. Maybe the guy panicked and got out of the car. Nobody saw anything. Everybody was watching the docking. Maybe the guy felt guilty, or thought he was responsible, so he walked off the ferry. We're checking the passenger list."

Just then, the Coast Guard guy and the investigator called over Chief Plutsky. He spoke to them in low tones. Then he walked back to us. "They traced the license plate," he said. "It was a rental. Now they're checking that out."

Joe nodded wearily. "Can we go, Jerry? I want to get Kate home. And we've told you all we can."

"Sure, Joe," Chief Plutsky said. "I'll keep you posted. Donny will give you a ride home in the cruiser. He already loaded your gear."

We all stood up and started toward the

door. Nick turned back. "Chief? Where was the car rented from?"

Chief Plutsky looked at the paper in his hand. "The Hartford airport," he said.

Nick hung back as Joe and Kate headed for the door. "There's your connection," he whispered to me. "Are you going to tell me now that nobody was following us?"

10//back in the saddle again

"Okay," I said to Nick when we got home. We sat in the family room, talking in low voices. "Let's go over this one more time. You're saying that the killer followed us all the way to Hartford—"

"Or they were on the same plane," Nick said. "They're connected to the Food Festival, or they work for the Cuisine Channel."

"Right," I said. "Some crazy chef murders a guy because he cheats him on some Cuban cigars. Then he rents a car at the airport and lurks outside long-term parking, waiting for a blue minivan full of the Annunciato family, and follows us to New London—"

"Everybody knows where Joe lives,"

Nick said. "The killer wouldn't even have to follow us. He rents a car and drives to the ferry and waits until we arrive. Then he quickly scoots in line behind us, so that his car will be behind ours."

"Pretty tricky maneuvering," I said.

"But not impossible," Nick argued.

"So why did he try to kill us?" I asked. "If we'd seen him, we would have told the police, and he'd know by now."

Nick ran both hands through his hair. "I don't know, Annie. Maybe he was trying to scare us. Maybe we know something that we don't *know* we know. You know?"

"No," I said. "This is crazy."

Just then we heard Joe's raised voice. He wasn't shouting, exactly. But it did sound as though he and Mom were arguing. Nick and I stopped talking and stared at each other. Joe and Mom never argued.

"I'm not being overprotective, I'm being sensible," Joe said. "And I wish you would be, too. You've just been through a traumatic exper—"

"Darling, I called the doctor." Mom's voice was lower, but we could still hear her.

"If he's not worried, why should we be?"

"Doctor?" I whispered. "What's going on?"

I hurried out of the family room, Nick on my heels.

"Listen, guys, if you want to have a private conversation, don't yell," Nick said.

"What's all this about a doctor?" I demanded. "Mom, are you okay?"

Joe and Mom looked at each other. I felt like I had swallowed a peach pit. Something hard and indigestible sat in my stomach.

"We didn't want to tell you—" Joe started.

"Tell us what?" I demanded.

"Yet," Joe continued. "Kate is going to have a baby."

Nick and I stared at Mom. Then we looked at Joe.

"I know, we're too old," Joe said. "But obviously, somebody up there didn't think so."

"But we're practically grown-up!" I protested. "You can't! I thought you were just getting fat, Mom!"

Mom looked amused. "Thanks, Annie." She came over to me and stroked my hair. "It was a surprise, but we're really happy," she said gently. "I hope you will be, too."

"A baby will turn the household upside down," Joe said. "No doubt about it. But I think we can handle it."

"I think it's great," Nick said. He hugged Mom, then hugged his father. "I'm going to have a real brother or sister."

I felt a pang in my heart. It was the way Nick had said "real." Of course, we weren't related by blood. But I'd thought we were as close as if we were.

"What am I, chopped liver?" I asked.

"Nah," Nick said. "You're more of a gefilte fish."

I couldn't even smile. I felt so strange. My whole world had shifted a half turn, just with a couple of words. Of course, I knew I was being selfish. I should have been happy Mom didn't have an awful disease. But I'd just gotten used to sharing Mom with Joe.

It always had been just me and Mom. My real dad had split for the wilds of Montana when I was three years old. I barely remembered having a dad. Now I'd have to learn how to have a baby sister or a brother. I was way too old for this.

"What do you say I cook up a big bowl of pasta tonight to celebrate?" Joe suggested. "We could all do with a night home. I'll run out to the store. And you," he said to Mom, "take a nap."

No wonder Joe had been so extra careful with Mom lately.

She kissed him lightly on the cheek. "I'm fine. But I think I will lie down for a few minutes."

Mom went upstairs, and Joe left for the store. Nick turned to me. "What's wrong?"

"Oh, nothing. You think somebody's trying to kill us, and we're about to be invaded by a puking, screaming baby. But I'm feeling perfectly swell," I said.

"I don't get it," Nick said. "Why aren't you thrilled? Most girls go ga-ga over babies."

"I'm not your average girl, okay?" I sounded sulky, but I didn't care.

"Yeah, I know that. But you've always said you missed having a sib growing up."

"I have all the sib I can handle at the moment," I said, eyeing him. "And I flunked sharing in kindergarten."

Nick gave me an exasperated look.

"It may sound like I'm being selfish," I said loftily, "but I'm only thinking of myself."

I couldn't brood about the new baby all weekend, not the way I wanted to. Nick wouldn't let me. He didn't listen to my whining, and he told me to grow up before there were two whining babies in the house. That's a quote.

Maybe he kept bringing up the murder as a diversion. Or maybe he really thought we could solve it. But Nick was determined to find out everything he could. "I say we pay a visit to Chief Plutsky," he said. "If we ask nicely, maybe he'll call the Key West police for us. Maybe they ID'ed the victim. Or maybe they traced that credit card and found out who rented the car."

"We are not exactly Chief Plutsky's favorite teens," I pointed out.

"What do you mean? He loves us," Nick said. "That tough, nasty exterior is just an act. Underneath it lies—"

"A tough, nasty interior," I finished.

I should mention that last Christmas, when Nick and I had solved the Three Fat Brothers Pizza Murder, Chief Plutsky hadn't been our biggest fan. He, along with Joe and Mom, had wanted to know the answers to such questions as, *Why didn't you contact the Scull Island police when you suspected Sal Peppino was a murderer?* and, *Why did you break into a suspected killer's house?* Little things like that.

"Secretly, he admires our detecting expertise," Nick said. "And besides, we've got no one else to ask. Let's go."

We grabbed our jackets and headed out. Scull Island is tiny, so the police station was within walking distance. *Everything* on Scull Island is walking distance. We stopped for a bag of doughnuts on the way. Nick thought it was overkill, but I suggested he remember Chief Plutsky's waistline. The man might be fighting calories, but the calories were winning.

Chief Plutsky groaned when he saw us come into the tiny Scull Island police station. He turned his back on us to pour himself a cup of coffee. "Don't tell me," he said.

"You discovered a clue. No. You discovered a body. No, wait—you realized that poking your nose into police business is a big mistake!"

Nick calmly ignored this. "Chief, we want you to know that we totally respect you," Nick said gravely. "Annie and I hold you in the highest esteem. In our minds, you're Columbo and Sherlock Holmes and Deputy Dawg rolled into one."

"Deputy Dawg?" Chief Plutsky repeated.

"That's why we're placing our trust, and our lives, in your capable, astute hands," Nick said.

Chief Plutsky sipped his coffee. "Enough of the snow job, kid. I've retired the dozers for the winter. What do you want?"

"Information," Nick said. "You may not know this, but Annie and I found a dead body in Key West."

"I heard," the chief said, sipping. "Big surprise."

Have I mentioned Scull Island is small? A piece of news gets around the island in three minutes flat.

"We think that murder might be connected to the ferry incident," I said.

He nodded, almost as though he were taking us seriously. That was a bad sign. Chief Plutsky never took us seriously. "Go on."

"So we were wondering if you'd call the Key West police and see if they have any new information," Nick continued. "When we left, they still hadn't identified the victim."

"Are you saying that the murderer followed you to Scull Island?" Chief Plutsky asked in disbelief.

"We're just saying it seems like an awfully big coincidence," Nick said carefully. "We get involved in a murder investigation in Key West—"

"Those poor cops," Chief Plutsky muttered.

"And then we almost get killed on the ferry," Nick finished. "Wouldn't *you* wonder, Chief Plutsky?"

He eyed us for a moment, weighing his options. He knew how persistent we could be. He probably didn't want to spend his Monday with us hanging around.

I held up the doughnut bag. "We brought doughnuts."

He sighed and picked up the phone. "I'm on a diet. Next time, bring fruit."

He located the number, then dialed it. He briefly explained who he was, and that there had been an accident involving two witnesses to a murder down there. He did more listening than talking. Nick and I waited, watching his face for clues. Not a muscle twitched. He made a few notes on a pad. Then he turned it over so that Nick couldn't peek.

"Okay, then," he said finally. "Appreciate it. If I can be of any help—yeah. Bye." He hung up.

"Well?" Nick prompted.

He put his hands together, as if he were praying. "If I give you two some information, will you promise to keep your nose out of this?"

"We promise," we chorused.

"Well, you can't get into any trouble up here," the chief said. "The investigation is focused in Key West and Miami."

"Miami? Why?" I asked.

"They identified the victim." Chief Plutsky turned over the pad. "One J. Bradley Binks, aka Brad Binks, aka John Bradley, aka Bradley Johns, aka Brad Hilton—in other words, a career criminal. Smuggler of various contraband, whatever fetches a good price."

"Brad Binks," Nick repeated.

"I always thought he looked like a criminal," I said.

The chief glanced at me curiously. "I thought you saw him when he was dead."

Oops. I shrugged. "He looked sleazy."

"What else?" Nick asked the chief. "I can tell there's something else."

Chief Plutsky sighed. "They found out where he was staying. They accessed the phone records and found out he'd made one call—to an airline." He consulted the pad. "Key Hoppers—"

"We flew that airline!" I said excitedly.

"And there was a notation on the pad—'310.' They figure he was meeting someone off a flight that got in at that time—3:10. Only one flight got in at that time that week, because it was delayed. It usually got in at 2:45. That flight was on the—"

"Eighteenth," Nick breathed. "We were on that flight!"

"With a murderer!" I cried.

Chief Plutsky slapped the pad on the desk. "Now how do you figure that?"

"It's obvious," I said. "Whoever he had gone to Key West to meet is who killed him. Nobody else knew him down there."

"Well, I guess that makes you two suspects," Chief Plutsky said with a sly grin. "They're checking the passenger list."

"Chief, did you ever find out any more about the rental car?" Nick asked.

"Yes." He crossed his arms.

"Aw, come on," Nick said. "You told us so much already."

He held up a finger. "This is the last thing, okay? The only reason I'm telling you is that this all seems to be connecting in Florida. Not here. Got it? Okay. The credit card used to rent the car belongs to a guy in Miami. Madison Folkes. His wallet was stolen in the Miami airport."

"Where we transferred to board our plane!" I said excitedly. "That means—"

But I stopped. Nick kicked me. And can I mention that it hurt?

"Thank you, Chief," he told Chief Plutsky. "You sure set our minds at rest."

I put the box of doughnuts on the desk. "Diets are for wimps."

We hurried out of the station. Outside, puffy white clouds danced in a baby-blue sky. Buds were opening on the trees, and daffodils were poking their cheerful yellow heads out of the cold ground in the town square. Danger and murder seemed very far away.

But I had been involved in a case where a guy had killed three people over pizza. I knew that murder could take place anywhere, even under puffy white clouds in a field of yellow daffodils.

"Nick, you were right," I said excitedly. "It all fits. The killer was on the same plane with us! They were on the Key Hoppers flight, and then the flight back to Hartford."

"Which means the killer is one of four people," Nick said, nodding. "Chip Waddell, Bob Summerhall, Marcia Fallows, or Parks McKenna."

"Whoever it was probably came up with a plan to get rid of us, or scare us," I said. "Each of those people knows we live on Scull Island. He—or she—stole a wallet in Miami so the police wouldn't be able to trace the rental car." I glanced around. "Which means—"

"The killer could be on Scull Island with us right now," Nick finished. He looked grim. "Waiting for another chance."

11//island trading

Under the circumstances, I decided it would be a really good idea to ride along with Joe when he drove Nick back to Manhattan the next day. Nick thought the killer probably wouldn't strike again, at least on Scull Island. It would look too suspicious. But I still wouldn't have minded trading islands for a day.

Besides, two of our suspects—Chip Waddell and Parks McKenna—lived in Manhattan. Joe had some meeting uptown, so Nick and I would be able to sneak away and do some fancy gumshoe footwork.

Joe talked about the new baby practically the whole way to Manhattan. I started to wonder if I should have stayed home and stared at the wall. It would have been ten times less boring than being in the car.

I was in the backseat and I tried to tune him out, but it was hard. Enthusiasm is tough to filter.

"I thought we'd paint that little sewing room," Joe said to me. "It would make a great nursery. Nobody in this family sews, anyway."

"I was thinking of learning," I said. Nick snorted.

"What do you say, Annie?" Joe asked. He looked at me in the rearview mirror. "Want to help me paint next weekend?"

"Awesome," I said. "Chores are my very favorite things to do on weekends. I was hoping you'd ask me."

"Don't mention it," Joe said cheerfully. My stepfather has one major flaw: He ignores sarcasm.

We sailed into Manhattan without getting snarled in a traffic jam, which is a minor miracle. Of course, Joe claimed it was his expertise, because he knew the best streets to use and how the lights were timed. He used to drive a cab in New York.

Joe parked in a lot near Nick's apartment. Nick slung his backpack and duffel over his shoulders, and we waited for Joe to pay the attendant.

"You could have been nicer about painting the nursery, you know," Nick said to me.

"I thought I sounded sufficiently eager," I said.

"You sounded like a selfish brat," Nick said.

I didn't say anything. Nick wasn't teasing. He wasn't trying to get my goat. He really meant it. That made me feel pretty awful.

So I didn't say a word on the short walk to Nick's apartment. Nobody seemed to notice, which made me feel even sorrier for myself.

Nick lives in a loft building that's been renovated, so instead of looking like a shabby warehouse, it looks like a swell warehouse. They've even hired a doorman to swank up the place.

As we approached the front door, Nick's footsteps slowed, and this totally goofy grin spread over his face. I followed his gaze to a tall, skinny girl at the entrance.

"Pia!" he cried.

Great. Just what I needed.

The girl turned around. She had very short, ebony-black hair. Her skin was very pale. She was wearing a navy crewneck sweater, jeans, and green suede loafers. Everything about her screamed Uptown Girl. Especially her tiny little nose.

"Nick!" Pia ran toward Nick. Nick ran toward Pia. It was a slow-mo perfume commercial.

They ran into each other's arms and hugged.

"I was going to call you the second I got in," Nick said.

"I couldn't wait, so I came down," Pia said.

Well, goo-goo ga-ga.

Grinning, Joe approached. "Let me take a wild guess. You must be Pia. I've only heard about, um, ten thousand things about you."

"Dad," Nick said, abashed.

Pia stuck out her bony hand. "I'm so glad to meet you, Mr. Annunciato. Pia Larkworthy."

And she had uptown manners, too.

She turned to me. Her eyes were Windex blue. "You must be Annie."

"I'm *so* glad to meet you," I said. "If Joe's heard ten thousand things about you, I must have heard a million!"

Pia laughed in an embarrassed way. "You must absolutely hate me," she said.

"Not at all," I lied.

Joe looked at his watch. "Listen, kids, would it be okay if I scoot out of here? I just have time to make my appointment uptown."

"Sure, Dad," Nick said. "Thanks for the lift home."

Joe tried to see his reflection in the glass-paned door. "How do I look? My agent said the Cuisine Channel is setting up an audition."

"You look swell," Nick said.

"Really handsome," I said.

"I'd watch you," Pia said.

"I'll meet you back here at three o'clock, Annie," Joe told me. "And don't be late. I want to beat the rush hour."

I promised I wouldn't. I was sorry to see Joe go. I almost asked if I could tag along.

Anything would be better than hanging around with the love bugs.

"Why don't I drop off my gear upstairs, and we can fill you in on the murder case?" Nick suggested to Pia.

"Sounds great," she said. "Are there any new developments?"

"You know about the murder?" I asked Pia as we walked to the elevator.

"Nick e-mailed me every night," Pia explained. "It's so fascinating."

"We figured we might nose around in the city today," Nick said. "Chip Waddell and Parks McKenna live here. Bob Summerhall lives in New Jersey, and Marcia has an apartment in Hartford and a summer place on Scull Island."

"Marcia seems your obvious suspect," Pia said. "I mean, she had the most reason to be on the ferry."

"Which is exactly why she's currently last on my list," Nick said. "It seems too obvious."

"Sometimes the obvious works," I said.

"And sometimes it doesn't," Nick said amiably. The elevator slid to a stop.

"Speaking of Chip Waddell, I think I might have a good clue," Pia said as we walked to the apartment door. "I just read in a gossip column today that he's opening a new restaurant."

"So?" I said.

"It's called Bluegrass," Pia explained. "And guess what—there's going to be a cigar bar attached to the restaurant."

Nick stopped dead. He dropped both his bags on the floor. "So Chip could have contacted Brad Binks about black market Cubans to sell to customers under the table!"

"And maybe he arranged to contact him on the Web site," I said. "Maybe Brad Binks thought at first you were Chip!"

"So Chip is the murderer?" Pia's blue eyes got round. "What do we do now? Go to the police?"

Nick and I grinned at each other. "Nah," I said. "We go see Chip."

12//where there's smoke

Chip turned out to be a company as well as a person. Waddell Productions was only five subway stops away, in midtown Manhattan.

We scanned the list posted in the lobby. The offices were on the fifth floor.

"How are we going to get in?" I wondered. "We can ask for Chip, but why would he want to see us?"

"Leave it to me," Pia said. "I'll get us in."

When we reached the offices, Pia strode right up to the receptionist. "Good morning," she said. "I'm Pia Larkworthy, David Larkworthy's daughter, from Tine-Worthy Press. I don't have an appointment, but I wonder if you could ask Mr. Waddell to give me just a few minutes."

Nick nudged me proudly. I had to admit

Pia was smooth. The receptionist didn't tell her to get lost, or even frost her a bit. She just picked up the phone. Pia looked so amazingly self-assured that the woman probably assumed she had a perfect right to be there.

"What's Tine-Worthy Press?" I whispered to Nick.

"A big publishing company," Nick whispered. "They publish three Nobel Prize winners."

"What does Pia's father do there?" I whispered.

"He owns it," Nick answered.

The receptionist put down the phone. "You can go right in, Ms. Larkworthy."

Pia signaled us, and we followed her into the office. The receptionist gave us a startled look, as though she didn't expect Pia to drag her raggedy friends along. But we just followed Pia's I-so-deserve-to-be-here lead.

Chip's office appeared much more sophisticated than he did. Everything was beige and black. Beige carpet, beige velvet sofa, black steel tables, black wood desk.

Chip looked like a big splash of catsup in his bright red shirt.

Pia strode toward him, her hand outstretched. "Pia Larkworthy, Mr. Waddell."

"Glad to meet you, young lady. How's your dad?" Chip focused his attention on Pia. He didn't even give us a glance, or look as though he remembered us.

"Daddy is well, thank you. I'll give him your regards," Pia said smoothly. "These are my very good friends, Nick Annunciato and Annie Hanley."

"Hey, I know you kids!" Chip pumped our hands heartily. His big red face looked friendly and puzzled, as though he were wondering what we were doing there. "I've only got a few minutes, so . . ."

"Let me tell you why we've barged in on you, Mr. Waddell," Pia said, flashing him a glimpse of perfect uptown teeth. "I'm in my senior year at Dalton, and we need a speaker for Career Day. I know I'm imposing, but Daddy thinks you're a genius—"

An expansive grin spread over Chip's face as he leaned against the desk. His belly flopped over his belt. The guy must love his own cooking.

"You're not imposing at all, hon," Chip said. "And I'd love to help you out. But with my show, and my new cookbook, and my new restaurant, my plate is full. My plate, get it? Just a little chef humor."

Pia laughed politely. "Your show is wonderful," she said warmly. "I love to watch it! I understand that you just taped a show in Key West." She tilted her head and fixed her bright blue eyes on Chip as though every word that barreled out of his mouth was pure wisdom. "What was that like?"

"I've gotta tell you, they loved me down there," Chip said enthusiastically. "And I was like a pig in slop. The South is Waddell country."

Chip went on to give Pia a blow-by-blow account of his activities at the Food Festival. What he cooked, how many people attended his book signing, what so-and-so said about his first cookbook. Big surprise: Chip Waddell turned out to be Chip Waddell's favorite subject.

"I'm thinking of going into TV production," Pia said. "This is all so incredibly fascinating to me. Tell me more about the taping."

"I introduced my new green chili hot sauce," Chip said. "Handed out advance jars. Every successful chef has to know about marketing himself." He reached behind him and took a jar labeled HOME-MADE SIN off the shelf. He handed it to Pia. "Here. A little present for you and your father. It's not even on the shelves yet. Enjoy."

Pia took the jar worshipfully, as though it were an Academy Award. "Thank you so much," she gushed. "I'm sure this is great. You are such a brilliant chef. Do they have internships at the Cuisine Channel, by any chance?"

"I don't know," Chip said. "I don't pay much attention to the tech side. I'm the talent."

"You certainly are. My father thinks you're brilliant, too," Pia said. "He said you're unhappy with your sales."

Chip looked eager. "I am. Sure, I'm a best-seller. But you can always improve your numbers. I'm not looking for a new publisher, you understand. Chip Waddell is *loyal*. But if somebody came calling, I'd give him a hearing." He winked at Pia.

"So how long did the taping last?" Pia asked.

"It went late—almost till eleven, I think," Chip said. "Don't think I don't work hard for my money. I cooked three different dishes with Homemade Sin. A chicken, a shrimp, and a—"

"What time did it end, exactly?" I asked. Chip looked annoyed at being interrupted. I realized I should have kept my mouth shut. But I was tired of all this chitchat.

"I don't know the precise time," Chip said frostily.

"Tell me about the third dish, Chip," Pia said, sending me a look that said, *Eat some paste, Annie. I'm handling this!*

I wasn't about to let Pia Not-worthy get away with that. "Is there any way you could find out?"

"It was eleven P.M.-ish, but I could check the video," Chip said in a sarcastic way. "That way I could tell you the exact *second* I finished the show."

"You have a timer on the video?" Nick asked.

Chip looked from Nick to me. "Hey," he said. "What's going on here?"

"I can't wait to taste this sauce," Pia said quickly. "Daddy and I will have some tonight."

Chip wasn't diverted. "Why are you so interested in how long my show ran?" he said to Nick and me. "Are you spying for your father? Is he getting a show on the Cuisine Channel? You tell him he can't copy Chip Waddell!"

Oops. Now we'd managed to get Joe in trouble.

"No!" I said quickly. "We're not spying for Joe. Not at all. Pia actually fibbed to you, Mr. Waddell. I'm the one who's interested in an internship at the channel. I was just too shy to say so. And since you're the star, I thought I'd come to you first. I figured I could get background info, so that when I go to the interview I could really impress them with my background knowledge."

"Well, I suppose I can understand that," Chip said. "I mean, if I were going for a job, I'd want me in my corner, too."

Nick shot me a look. We knew each other so well that I knew what he was telling me: *Good save, Annie. But stop there.* So I did.

A buzzer went off on his phone, and Chip picked it up. "Who? Oh, sure. Send her in."

"If that's all, I've got an interviewer coming in," Chip said to us. "So—"

"Sure. We'll get out of your hair," Pia said.

The door opened, and Marcia Fallows walked in. "Chip! Thanks for arranging that tasting at Bluegrass. I adored every single thing I tasted," Marcia gushed. "Especially that chili cream sauce for the pork."

"I haven't reduced it yet," Chip told her.

"Who cares about calories when it's so delicious!" Marcia trilled. Then, she noticed us standing by the door. "Hello—it's Mick and . . . Bonnie, isn't it?"

"Nick and Annie," Nick said.

"Right. Chip, I tried that Homemade Sin sample last night that I got at your taping—I made the chicken dish you showed us in Key West. It was sublime."

"You were at Chip's taping?" I asked Marcia.

"Of course," she said. "I'm doing an article on him."

"Don't you kids have to be somewhere?" Chip asked pointedly.

We said good-bye and split. Nobody spoke until we hit the sidewalk.

"Two strikes," Nick said with a sigh. "Chip couldn't have killed Brad Binks. He's got an ironclad alibi."

"And Marcia was with him," I said.

"You were fantastic," Nick said to Pia. He slung an arm around her shoulders. "You have a flair for this, girl."

Pia grinned. "It was fun."

"I couldn't believe how you wound Chip around your little finger," Nick said. "You got every drop of information out of him."

Excuse me? I was the one who provoked him into telling us about the video timer that would clear him for sure!

"Maybe we should check out that video, just to confirm they were both telling the truth," Nick said. "What do you think, Pia?"

Pia? Was I invisible? Had I become Nick's silent partner?

She nodded. "Might not be a bad idea. We'd have to figure out how to do it without Chip suspecting something."

"I'm sure you'll figure that out," Nick said admiringly. "Okay. Next stop, Bob Summerhall and Parks McKenna."

"My dad had to investigate an employee who he suspected of embezzling from his company," Pia said. "He found out all kinds of stuff, just from this LEXIS-NEXIS service he has. I could enter McKenna and Summerhall and see what I can find."

"Excellent!" Nick beamed at Pia. It was like she had just become one of her father's Nobel Prize winners. And I had fallen through the sidewalk and disappeared. I was floating in the New York City sewer system, approaching the Hudson River, where I would drift out to sea and be lost forever. When they'd told Nick I was gone, he'd say, *Annie who?*

"Isn't she a genius?" Nick asked, still gazing at Pia.

"A regular Einstein," I said. "Harvey Einstein, our plumber? Boy, does he know toilets."

Nobody heard me. Nick and Pia were already walking toward the subway, hand in hand.

Annie who?

13//wired in

you've got mail!

To: sohopunk@cyberspace.com

(Nick Annunciato)

From: outRAGme@cyberspace.com

(Annie Hanley)

Re: Suspect Bob

Scratch another suspect. Bob Summerhall was at Joe's cooking demo. We figure the murder was committed somewhere between 8:10 and 8:20, right? Joe's demo was cut short because the police called to tell him we were at the station. He cancelled the demo at about 8:50. He remembers Bob S. being there until he was. So there's no way Bob could have done the evil deed.

Has Miss Stick come up with any leads? Given her genius brilliance, that is.

To: outRAGme@cyberspace.com

(Annie Hanley)

From: sohopunk@cyberspace.com

(Nick Annunciato)

Re: more on Bob

ok, so Bob-a-lu isn't a suspect. but guess what? I called him, pretending to be doing research on Tunisia for a school paper— remember, he's Mr. Mediterranean? he told me that down in key west, somebody stole his chef knives from his luggage. and carved up some tenderloin-de-hand, maybe? the police in fla are checking out the connection. Ze plot, she thickens. . . .

pia is not a stick. she is PERFECTION. she's working on McKenna research at the mo. nothing to go on yet—his address isn't listed, so she's digging on the Net.

To: sohopunk@cyberspace.com

(Nick Annunciato)

From: outRAGme@cyberspace.com

(Annie Hanley)

Re: nada zilch squat

Tried to pump Chief Plutsky, but he

kicked me out. I even brought him some Florida grapefruit!

How do you feel about yellow? I used to like the color. But now that I'm painting the nursery, I'm seeing it all day. I'm inhaling it. I'm dreaming it. I'm hating it. Why is there yellow? The question haunts me.

To: outRAGme@cyberspace.com

(Annie Hanley)

From: sohopunk@cyberspace.com

(Nick Annunciato)

Re: there's always room for yellow

listen, brat. enough already. i happen to be a fan of yellow. and Joe needs the help, so get back to work. i'll come out next weekend and help, if you want.

my adorable girlfriend came up with some major news on Parks McK. he's shopping a cookbook deal all over town. this is the news according to Dear Old Dad, David Larkworthy, who got a proposal. editors aren't jumping on it—apparently, our Parks handled the business end of the Waddell-McKenna partnership when they *had that restaurant. they call Parks a "front of the house" person in the food biz. Chip handled all the food, so nobody actually knows if Parks can cook.*

i'm not sure how all this ties in, but it's good info. pia's going to tackle chip again. can you think of any questions she should ask?

```
To: sohopunk@cyberspace.com
(Nick Annunciato)
From: outRAGme@cyberspace.com
(Annie Hanley)
Re: some questions
```

So Miss Brilliant Stick needs my help? Glad to oblige.

Question #1: What was on Chip's hard drive in his laptop? The one that was stolen in Fla.

Question #2: Was Parks at Chip's taping?

That's all I can think of at the mo. Joe is calling. I'm seeing yellow in my future. Let me know the skinny from the Stick.

To: outRAGme@cyberspace.com

(Annie Hanley)

From: sohopunk@cyberspace.com

(Nick Annunciato)

Re: the chipster comes through

here's the skinny: chip kept all his recipes on his hard drive. and parks was at the taping, but chip doesn't remember when he arrived, or when he left, and pia didn't want to push it.

oh, chip invited pia and her father out to the cuisine channel studios. obviously a ploy to snare a book contract. But if pia goes, she can check out that tape.

There was no way, José, I was going to let Miss Stick do my detecting for me. If Pia checked out the tape, she'd get major credit. I'd had enough of Pia taking over. I was back in charge.

I signed off Nick's e-mail and headed into the nursery. Joe was whistling while he painted the woodwork.

"I've come to your aid, Kemo Sabe," I said.

"Hi ho, Silver," Joe said. "Grab a brush."

As I dipped my brush in paint, I noticed a baby monitor on the table. "Uh, Joe? I don't think you really need to monitor an empty room, do you? Plenty of time before the baby arrives."

"Your mom got a box of old baby stuff from her friend Jennifer," Joe explained while he swished. "I set it up so that I can paint and cook at the same time. I'm working on my recipes for my audition. This way I can hear the oven buzzer downstairs."

"What a Renaissance guy," I said. "Joe, didn't you tell me that your audition for the Cuisine Channel is tomorrow?"

"Yeah," Joe said, nodding. "But I feel totally prepared. How tough can it be? All I have to do is cook and talk, two things I happen to be very good at."

"I was wondering if I could tag along," I said. "I won't get in your hair. It's just that I've never been to a television studio before. I could probably impress my best friend Rochelle and all the goons at school when I go back."

"Impress them with a cable channel?" Joe looked skeptical. "It's not exactly MTV."

"She's not exactly Madonna," I said.

"Well, okay, then," Joe said, dipping his brush in paint and dripping it on his pants. "You can help me stay relaxed in the car."

"I'll tell you the story of my life," I said. "That should put you to sleep."

Joe laughed. I went to attack the windowsills with my paintbrush. Take that, Pia Larkworthy! Nobody gets the jump on Annie Hanley. Not even with those long legs.

14//all in the timing

That afternoon, I left six messages for Chip Waddell. Finally, when I called at seven, he took the call.

"I promise I will never call you again, or show up at your office, if you give me permission to look at the Key West tape," I told him. "I'm doing a report for school, and it would be so awesome to throw around technical terms."

There was a long pause. "You won't bother me again?"

"Never. I swear."

A long, deep sigh. "Okay. I'll call the tech person, what's-his-name, and put you on a list or whatever."

"Thank you sooo—" I started, but Chip had already hung up.

@   @   @

In the overhead fluorescent lights of the Cuisine Channel hallway, Joe's skin looked almost green.

He tugged at his collar. "No problem. No problem at all. It's a piece of cake."

"Not cake," I teased. "You're making pasta. Remember?"

Joe looked glassy-eyed. "Are you sure you're okay?" I asked.

"Maybe I shouldn't have made huevos rancheros for breakfast," Joe said. "The jalapeño peppers are killing me."

"You'll be fine," I assured him. "You're a master chef and a master talker. Remember? You're gold. You're a champion. You're solid. Now get out there and win, win, win!" I thumped him on the back with each *win*.

"Right," Joe said. "What am I cooking, again?"

A dazed Joe walked off to the studio to meet his fate. I headed for one of the editing rooms, where a tech person had agreed to meet me.

Wally Skimmer wore a PLAYS WELL WITH OTHERS T-shirt and a sour expression.

Despite the shirt, he did not look happy to see me. But all I had to say was, "Chip sent me," and Wally waved me in. Lucky for *moi,* here at the Cuisine Channel, what Chip Waddell wants, Chip Waddell gets.

"So I'm supposed to cue up the tape we shot in Key West, right?" Wally asked me. He leaned so far back in his chair, I thought he might tumble over.

"If it's not too much trouble," I said sweetly.

Wally gave an exaggerated sigh. Then he reached for a tape, stuck it in the machine, and pressed "play." After such an effort, I wondered if he'd have to take a coffee break.

He showed me how to use the "pause" button and "rewind" and "fast forward." It really wasn't much more complicated than a VCR, but Wally made it sound as though he worked for NASA.

Chip appeared on the screen, dressed in the blue gingham shirt and denim apron that was his trademark. The show hadn't begun yet, and he was greeting some members of the audience. I saw Marcia chatting

up Chip, and Parks lingering in the back. I
noted the timer: 6:56. I wrote the number
on a pad, and wrote "Marcia" and "Parks"
next to it.

I then proceeded to watch an extremely
boring cooking demonstration. Boring for
me, that is. The audience loved Chip, and
shouted "Hot stuff!" whenever he waved a
pepper at them.

Chip had lied about one thing. His show
began at about 7:10, not 8:00 P.M., as he'd
said. It could have been an innocent mistake, but I wrote a big question mark next
to his name, to remind me to mention it to
Nick.

I was watching the master tape, which
included shots from three separate cameras.
That was lucky, because there was probably
more panning of the audience on this tape
than there would be on the final, edited version. When the piece actually aired, I was
sure Chip would have more than his share
of close-ups. I fast-forwarded through all of
those.

"Good move," Wally grunted. He
reached underneath the console and took

out a paper bag. He unwrapped a burger and bit into a Big Mac. When I'd first arrived in the editing room, I'd thought I smelled cheeseburgers, but the whole station smelled like food. My stomach had started rumbling as soon as I'd hit the reception desk.

"I hope nobody here at Gourmet Central sees you eating McFood," I said.

He grinned and held out his French fries. "I won't tell if you won't."

I munched on Wally's fries as I watched the tape. As Chip prepared a "scallion tomatillo salsa that will knock your huaraches off," the camera panned the audience again.

Marcia's seat was empty! Although at the start of the broadcast she'd been right up front, she'd moved to a seat in the back after Chip had begun to cook. Which was weird, if you thought about it, since she was doing an article on him. I wrote down the time: 7:12. Way early for the murder, but I'd watch for her return.

The camera caught Marcia slipping back into her seat at 7:36. I wrote down the time.

It was probably a bathroom break, or a cigarette break.

Marcia stayed in her seat for the remainder of the show, so that let her out as a suspect. But Parks left at 8 P.M. and never came back at all!

"Bingo," I breathed. Since Brad Binks had been killed around 8:15, that made Parks a definite suspect.

But what was his motive? The only thing I could figure was that he was trying to hurt Chip somehow. What if he'd arranged with this sleazy smuggler to import bad cigars for Chip's cigar bar? Reputation was everything in the New York restaurant world. Word of mouth could ruin Chip's new business.

I was so excited that it was hard to keep watching the tape. But I had to make sure that Parks never came back.

The show ended at 10:13. The audience went up to the counter to eat what Chip had prepared. Parks wasn't there.

Chip had said that the show ended at eleven. He had lied about the time, but I didn't think it mattered. Maybe he got mixed up because he taped his show at different times in the studio.

The good news was, we had a definite suspect. It was time to find out everything we could about Parks McKenna.

15//clue crazy

It took Joe the entire ride back to New London to get over himself. Apparently, he had not made a stellar audition tape.

"I saw that red light go on, and I developed this stutter," he said in amazement as we waited in the car for the ferry to dock. "A-and n-now f-f-folks, I'm going to t-take this onion and . . ." Joe stopped.

"And?" I prompted.

"And nothing," Joe said mournfully. "I forgot the word for 'sauté.' Sauté, Annie! I blanked. I stood there, holding the onion, and my eyes started to tear. From the onion, but who knew? I have been humiliated. I should fall on my sword, or my chef's knife, or whatever those fall-on-their-sword guys do."

"There, there," I said, patting his arm. Sometimes adults need child care. I swear.

"I have one consolation," Joe said. "Nobody will ever see that tape."

"Unless it shows up on one of those blooper shows," I pointed out.

Joe closed his eyes in pain. "Thanks, Annie."

The ferry guy began signaling us to drive onto the platform. I was glad to see that this time, we weren't in front. I was still a little edgy about the ferry experience.

"That Cuisine Channel is some state-of-the-art facility," I said. "I guess the stakes are pretty high in the food biz these days."

"It's a huge industry," Joe agreed. "I just basically scrape along, but somebody like Chip Waddell makes millions. If you put it together, the books, shows, products, personal appearances—don't you love that phrase, Annie? I mean, every appearance is personal, isn't it?— it all really adds up."

"Do you think the stakes are high enough that people would, you know, lie, cheat, and steal to get ahead?" I asked him.

Joe parked the car and set the emergency brake. "People lie, cheat, and steal when stakes are *low*, Annie. But, yeah, I guess so."

We got out of the car and started toward the top deck. "Because I've heard that Parks and Chip aren't so friendly," I continued.

"I've heard that, too," Joe said. "But I don't know the details. I'm out of the loop."

"Maybe Parks is jealous of Chip's money," I said. "If Chip makes millions, what happened to Parks? Why would one chef make it big, and another one just scrape by? TV exposure? The right agent?"

Joe paused by the railing. The wind whipped his dark hair in his eyes as he gave me a searching glance. "What's this about, Annie?"

Whoa. Back up, Annie. If Joe found out I was still investigating, he'd have about two conniptions and lock me in my room with bread and water. Well, knowing Joe, home-made sourdough and Perrier. I'd have to come up with something good. The problem was, something good just doesn't tend to occur to me when a parent is giving me the fish-eye.

"Nothing," I said, shrugging. Maybe the teen response would head him off at the pass.

"Is this about the baby?" Joe asked.

What? Talk about left field! "The baby?" I asked cautiously.

"Are you worried that the new baby will cost too much money?" Joe asked. "I'm not a megabucks chef, but we're doing okay. Your mom is taking off about six weeks, but then she's going to freelance from home. We worked it all out."

I started to tell Joe that I wasn't worried about money, but I stopped. If I wasn't worried about the baby, why was I asking him those questions?

"If you're worried about college, your mom and I have talked about it," Joe went on. "We want you to know we'll swing it, no matter what you decide. We have money saved, and we can take out a loan."

Now I felt really terrible. Joe thought I was being totally selfish! Of course I *had* been feeling selfish about the baby, but it wasn't about money. I was needy, not greedy.

He slung his arm around my shoulders and gave me a quick hug. "So don't worry. We've got it covered."

It was a total drag to have my cool

stepfather think I was a selfish, greedy brat. But what else could I do?

Just then, I saw Marcia Fallows on the lower deck. She was standing with a tall, reedy guy with a long face and a truly pathetic mustache. As a subject changer, it would do nicely.

"Look, there's Marcia," I said. "Let's go say hi."

Joe and I headed down to the lower deck. Marcia didn't look all that pleased to see us. "Oh, right, you live on Scull Island," she said. "We're going over to open up the house for the season. This is my boyfriend, Dr. Richard Tell."

He nodded at us. His palm was damp when I shook it. You had a feeling that Dr. Tell was not exactly the sparkling star of the social circuit. I couldn't imagine what Marcia was doing with such a nerdy, loser-type guy. She was more the city-glam type.

"Ah, just what I need, a doctor," Joe said jovially. "Dr. Tell, what would you say about a person who suddenly develops a stutter and forgets his own name?"

"I wouldn't know," he said.

"Dick is a scientist, not a medical doctor," Marcia explained.

"Oh, interesting," Joe said. "Do you work nearby?"

"Yes," the scintillating Dr. Dick replied.

"And what kind of work do you do?" Joe pressed on. The trouble with my stepfather is that he is genuinely interested in people.

"Sheep," Dr. Dick said. "I work with sheep."

"On a farm?" I asked, puzzled.

"In a laboratory," he said. "I work on diseases that affect livestock."

"Oh, you must work on Blackberry Island?" Joe said, and Dr. Dick gave a short nod.

Blackberry Island is this tiny island not far from Scull Island. There's a government animal research facility there, and KEEP OUT signs are posted everywhere. No one is allowed to land a boat there, or even get within a few hundred yards of shore. It's patrolled by government boats. Naturally all the kids on Scull Island are convinced that top-secret, sci-fi chilling experiments are being conducted there. We used to scare each other at slumber parties talking about two-headed cows and vampire sheep. We'd picture them breaking out of their pens and swimming to Scull Island, where they would invade our house, raid our slumber party, and bite off our heads.

"Wow," I said. "Do you really breed two-headed cows there?"

"Annie, behave yourself," Joe said. He turned back to Dr. Dick. "So, do you?"

"No," Dr. Dick said.

Joe grinned. "You've got to know about the reputation of that place. Every time a hurricane brews out in the Atlantic, a couple of crazies on Scull Island start this whole doom-and-gloom scenario, where some sort of contamination will blow over from the facility, like hoof-and-mouth disease, or—"

"That reminds me, Joe," Marcia interrupted. "Do you put meat in your chili?"

Joe turned to Marcia, amused. "Nice segue, Marcia. Why do you ask?"

Marcia swept back a lock of her hair. She wore a thick gold band with scrollwork on her third finger. It almost looked like a wedding ring, but it was on the wrong hand. "I just wrote an article on chili for *Foodstuff* magazine," Marcia explained. "I did a ton of research on regional differences. At the end of the article, the magazine wants me to ask chefs for their favorite ways to cook chili. It's a regular feature of their articles. I've done so many articles for these people, you'd think they'd give me a break and do the phone work themselves. What's your secret, Joe?"

"Chipotles," Joe said.

"Ah," Marcia said. "So you use a mixture of beans."

"Chipotle peppers," Joe said. "That's what gives it that smoky flavor. No meat, just black beans. I'm not a chili purist, either. I always set out toppings—grated cheddar, chopped onion, cilantro."

"Sounds delicious," Marcia said. But she didn't seem to be paying attention anymore.

"I really like it when Joe makes Cincinnati chili," I put in.

Marcia nodded knowingly.

"I thought it was a totally weird idea at

first," I said. "But if you can serve chili over rice, why not?"

"Mmmm," Marcia said, running a hand through her tight blond ringlets. "I love chili over rice. I'd never second-guess Cincinnati."

Since Joe has become my stepfather, I have become your basic cookbook index. I know about twenty different ways to fix pasta, for example. I also know that Cincinnati chili is famous for being served over spaghetti, not rice. Marcia pretended that she knew, but she didn't. If she was such a food expert, shouldn't she know that?

I thought it was time to swing the conversation around to the suspects. More information-gathering was in order. And who better to pump for info than the journalist who was writing an article on Chip? I bet Marcia knew plenty about the Parks-Chip feud.

"Speaking of chili, Chip Waddell is famous for his hot sauces," I said. "Do you think they're any good, Marcia?"

"They're fabulous," Marcia said. "I'm a big Waddell fan."

"What about Parks McKenna?" I asked.

"What about him?" Marcia replied.

"Do you think he's a good chef?"

Marcia shrugged. "Chip says Parks doesn't know how to cook more than the basics. But I'm staying away from that feud."

"So they *are* feuding," I said.

"Well, let me just say this," Marcia said. She leaned in closer. "Parks is not Chip's favorite person. I understand Parks hasn't forgiven Chip for getting him fired from his show. You know that Parks produced it in the beginning, right? But when Chip got famous, Parks couldn't handle it. At least, that's what Chip says."

"What a business," Joe said. "I should go into something safe, like dismantling land mines."

Just then, we heard a child's cry from behind us. A kid about three years old had dropped a snow globe and must have reached down to pick it up. His hand looked as though it was cut pretty badly. The child's mother picked him up, but obviously didn't know what to do next.

Before any of us could move, Marcia

sprang forward. "Can I help?" she asked the mother in a calm voice.

"I-I don't know," the mother said distractedly. She tried to wrap the hem of her T-shirt around her child's wound to stop the flow of blood.

"Annie, run for napkins!" Marcia directed crisply as she knelt in front of the child. "Joe, there's got to be a first-aid kit onboard. See if you can find one."

"What should I do?" Dr. Dick asked nervously. "I'm not an MD, but—"

"Just stay out of the way," Marcia barked.

Joe and I took off. I ran to the snack bar and came back with a wad of napkins. Moments later, Joe and a ferry worker returned with the first-aid kit.

"Everything is going to be okay," Marcia told the mother soothingly as she bandaged the wound with gauze and tape. "It doesn't look bad at all. He'll be just fine."

I stood back, watching. Some murder suspect—Marcia clucked and cooed at the kid while she reassured the mother. She disinfected and dressed the wound quickly and gently, like a professional mom. If I'd ever imagined there was a glint of possible evil in her green eyes, the image faded.

And so did my chance to pump for more information on Parks McKenna.

To: outRAGme@cyberspace.com

(Annie Hanley)

From: sohopunk@cyberspace.com

(Nick Annunciato)

Re: number one suspect

nice work, Annie. but aren't we supposed to clear any field trips with each other? it's a good thing pia didn't decide to go after the tape—you two would have overlapped. chip would have gotten suspicious.

anyway. parks looks like our guy, but we need more. pia has been on the case. she used that fancy search engine of Dear Old Dad's and found out his unlisted address. we tailed him for a couple days, and guess what? the guy heads out with a paper bag, goes to a lab, and hands it over for analysis. it's the kind of place that will analyze stuff for a fee. go figure.

but here's the real news. our guy lives in a building right across the street from Mr. Larkworthy's publishing company! we scoped it out, and you can see into his kitchen window from one of the offices. pia borrowed this fancy-schmantzy camera from some kid at school whose father is some kind of paparazzo. it's got this incredible telescopic lens. we can sneak in the bldg after hours and do some truly high-tech surveillance.

as holmes would say, the game's afoot, watson!

```
To: sohopunk@cyberspace.com
(Nick Annunciato)
From: outRAGme@cyberspace.com
(Annie Hanley)
Re: you gotta be kidding
```

Totally dumb idea. Snooping could get us in major trouble. Isn't it illegal, first of all? And doesn't the publishing co have security? Miss Stick doesn't seem so brilliant after all.

To: outRAGme@cyberspace.com
(Annie Hanley)
From: sohopunk@cyberspace.com
(Nick Annunciato)
Re: green monster

you don't like the idea because it's Pia's. get over yourself, annie! we're going wednesday night.

To: sohopunk@cyberspace.com
(Nick Annunciato)
From: outRAGme@cyberspace.com
(Annie Hanley)
Re: wednesday

I am not jealous. It is a dumb idea. I'm coming along.

16 // i spy

I took the train to New York City, and Nick met me at Penn Station. I have to admit it was good to see him. Detecting on your own can feel lonely, even with e-mail.

"Where's your shadow?" I asked him. Then I could have cheerfully kicked myself. Nick's smile turned into a scowl. If I know what I'm about to say is stupid and childish, why do I say it?

"She's in the bathroom," he said. "Look, Annie, can you lighten up on Pia? You're really running on my last nerve."

"Okay," I said grudgingly. Nick was right, but that didn't make it any easier to agree.

Pia glided out of the rest room, managing to look elegant in the middle of a public waiting room. Underneath her navy blazer, she was wearing a white T-shirt and blue jeans, just like I was. How did she manage to look so chic? I wondered if this was the first time she'd been in an actual train station. She was more of a limousine gal.

"Hi, Annie," she said. "How was the trip?"

"Uneventful," I said. "Are we set for tonight?"

Nick nodded. "Pia borrowed her dad's security pass."

She grinned. "Only he doesn't know it."

"Subway?" Nick asked.

Pia shuddered. "Can we take a cab this time? I really hate the subway."

What a wimp! I didn't look at Nick, or even say an unkind word. I was improving my character every second.

I hefted my backpack on one shoulder, and we started toward the escalators.

"I forgot to tell you about Marcia," I said. "I know she has an alibi, but she isn't the experienced food journalist that she claims to be. She didn't know what a chipotle pepper is, or what Cincinnati chili is."

Nick nodded thoughtfully. "That reminds me. Remember at Chip's office, when he said a sauce needed to be reduced?"

"You're right!" I exclaimed. "She thought he meant cut the calories."

"So did I," Pia said. "What does reducing a sauce mean?"

"It means simmering it or boiling it until it gets more concentrated," Nick explained.

We hit Seventh Avenue and joined the line for taxicabs.

"Anyway, that made me suspicious, so I did a search on the Net," I said. "The magazine Marcia said she writes for all the time is on the Net and has archives. When I plugged in her name, nothing came up. Doesn't that seem weird?"

"Sure," Pia said with a shrug. "But not criminal. She was probably exaggerating her credentials to impress you. Everybody does that."

"But in a murder case, every lie is significant," Nick said.

"Okay, we have some extra time," Pia said. "Daddy won't be home for hours. Why don't we log on to his computer and do some more digging on Marcia?"

@   @   @

Pia lives in total swank. Her apartment is huge, with ceiling-high windows that face Central Park. There are bookshelves crammed with books in every room. Books are even stacked in columns on the floor.

"Daddy's work is also his hobby," Pia explained, waving at the array of books. "Mom lives in Paris," she said to me. "She's working on a book about the relationship between Picasso and Matisse. Really fascinating stuff."

"I always thought so," I said.

"They're separated, but they're working it out," Pia said. "How they can work out a relationship when one person lives in Paris and one lives in New York, don't ask me. But nobody ever asks me."

For a moment, a lost look flitted over Pia's face. Poor little rich girl. But it was hard for me to feel sympathy for someone with her wardrobe.

We logged on to the computer in her dad's study. Pia accessed the search engine, and we spent a good hour looking up everything we could on Marcia Fallows.

It was strange. She's a journalist, but she started out as a general reporter in Portland, Oregon. We scanned a list of her articles, and it looked like she'd written on everything *but* food. Then she'd gotten a job as the science reporter on a Hartford newspaper. She'd resigned just three months ago.

"That must be how she met Dr. Dick," I said.

"She's written a whole bunch of articles," Nick said as he scrolled. He glanced at the computer clock. "But we don't have time to look at them."

"I'll print out the list," Pia offered. "We can look at them later, if we get stuck on the case. Who knows, something weird might turn up."

Pia printed out the list, and I stuffed it in my backpack. Then we took off for Operation: Parks.

Pia breezed by security with her dad's ID with no problem. She spun a story about printing off some files from his computer, explaining that we might be there for several hours.

Maybe the girl had a talent for detection, after all. Being a detective often involves a flair for deceit. I'm not very good at it, but Nick is a whiz. I was beginning to see that Pia was, too. Maybe they *were* meant for each other.

We found the office that Nick and Pia had already scoped out. Parks's kitchen window was dark. Pia set up the camera on the tripod.

"Now, we wait," Nick said.

At first, it was kind of thrilling to be sitting in an empty office building, waiting for something to happen. But pretty soon, staring at a dark window got a tad dull.

"What if he's out for the night?" I asked. "Did anyone think of trying to check on that?"

"How would we do that?" Nick asked crankily.

"Ask Pia," I said. "She's the genius."

My sarcasm was lost on Pia. "I guess I should have thought of that. You're right, Annie. This could be a complete waste of—"

"Heads up," Nick breathed. The kitchen light had gone on.

Nick and I both sprang for the camera at the same time. We cracked heads. Nick fell back with an *"Ow!"* and I took my place behind the lens.

"Wow!" I whispered. "I can practically see his nostril hairs. This lens is incredible."

But after I'd gotten used to the view, I had to admit there wasn't much to see. Parks sat at the kitchen table in his shirt-sleeves. He opened his laptop. The cover was facing me, so I couldn't read anything on the screen. Then he turned on the TV.

"The Cuisine Channel, of course," I said.

I have to let you in on something here. Surveillance isn't fun. You'd think it would be, in an *I Spy*, cloak-and-daggerish way. But it's actually about as much fun as watching paint dry. I should know.

"He's cooking something," Pia observed. It was her turn at the camera. "And he's making notes."

"Probably working on the cookbook he can't sell," I said. "This is totally fascinating."

When it was my turn at the lens, I watched Parks make a chicken dish. I watched him measure olive oil, chop garlic and green olives, and sauté onions.

"You know what, Nick?" I said. "He doesn't cook like a chef. Look."

Nick put his eye against the lens. "Clumsy chopping technique. And the flame is too high under the pan. He's going to burn the onions."

"All this food-watching is making me hungry," I groaned. "Why didn't we think to bring a sandwich or something?"

Pia hefted her leather shoulder bag from the floor. She reached in and took out a brown paper bag. Then she reached in and took out a colorful dish towel. She spread it on the desk, then unwrapped sandwiches and pickles.

"No dessert?" I said.

With a smile, she reached into her bag and brought out a wrapped bundle of cookies.

"Homemade," she said. "My housekeeper is a genius cookie baker."

"Is everybody you know a genius?" I asked her.

But I have to admit that, despite appearances, Pia was actually interested in ingesting food.

After we'd wolfed the sandwiches, chomped on the pickles, and washed down the cookies with the small bottle of Evian Pia drew from her amazing bottomless purse, we had to watch Parks again.

"This is getting us exactly nowhere," Nick complained. "I say we kick-start this scenario."

He turned on the computer at the desk. "Good, he has the same online service," he muttered. "I can log on as a guest."

"What are you doing?" Pia asked.

"Didn't you get his e-mail address?" Nick asked her.

"Sure. It was on the book proposal he sent Daddy," Pia said. "Hang on, I wrote it in my notebook."

Leave it to Pia to buy a notebook just to record her observations and clues on the case. Naturally, it was one of those little handmade paper jobs that cost you an arm and a leg.

"It's 'Parksfood@cyberspace.com,'" Pia read out. "What are you going to say, Nick?"

"It's a little ploy Annie and I used in the

pizza murders," Nick explained. "When you don't know if the bear is sleeping, poke him with a stick."

Pia gave me a puzzled look. I shrugged. We both looked over Nick's shoulder.

```
To: Parksfood@cyberspace.com
From: sohokid@cyberspace.com
Re: I know what you did, fella
```

Don't think you can get away with it. I'm following your every move. I know what you did and who you are, and the cover-up isn't working. Got it? Good. I'll be in touch.

"Not very original," I pointed out.

"But let's hope it's effective," Nick said. He twirled around in the chair and put his eye to the camera lens. "Nothing so far."

"Maybe his program doesn't tell him he has e-mail," Pia said.

"Who knows when he'll check," I said. "I mean, we teens check every two seconds. But adults aren't as electronically needy."

Nick looked crushed that his scheme didn't fly. "He's got to see the letter sometime," he muttered. "Unless . . ." He began to fiddle with the focus. "How do I zoom in with this, Pia?"

"Like this," she said, showing him.

"Holy Toledo," Nick breathed. "The laptop doesn't belong to Parks! It's Chip Waddell's! I can see the ID label pasted on the cover."

"So Parks is the one who stole Chip's laptop!" I said.

"And now he's stealing Chip's recipes," Pia said. "His notes for his cookbook are on his hard drive. That's why Parks is making notes and trying to cook. He's a cook crook!"

"And maybe a murderer," Nick said.

Just then, the office lights blazed on. We all jumped about five feet in the air. A handsome, gray-haired man in sweat clothes stood in the doorway.

"Daddy!" Pia exclaimed.

David Larkworthy frowned. "What are you doing here, young lady? Where's my ID?" His sharp gaze went from Nick to me to the camera trained on the building across the courtyard. "And what are you doing?"

"Before I tell you, can we turn out the lights?" Pia begged.

"It's too late," Nick said. We all looked across the courtyard. Parks stood at the window, staring at us across the space.

"He saw us," Nick said.

17//busted

"What is going on here?" Mr. Larkworthy roared.

We turned back to him.

"You see, Daddy—" Pia started.

"I know how this looks, Mr. Larkworthy—" Nick began in his lowest, most sincere tone.

"We haven't been introduced, but—" I started.

Mr. Larkworthy wasn't listening. He looked over our heads. "What the . . ."

We turned. Parks was holding up a sign. It was too far away to read. Mr. Larkworthy strode to the camera and bent his tall frame over the viewfinder. When he looked back at us, his face was grim.

"What is it?" Pia asked nervously.

"Why don't you kids have a look?" Mr.

Larkworthy suggested in a voice that could melt a polar ice cap.

I was closest, so I bent down and looked through the viewfinder. I could see the hair on Parks's knuckles, and the texture of his skin as he held up the sign:

IF I DON'T GET AN EXPLANATION, I'M CALLING 911.

"Perhaps," Mr. Larkworthy suggested, "we should take a stroll across the street."

"I don't know if that's such a good idea," Nick hedged.

"I don't think you have a choice," Mr. Larkworthy replied. "March."

We marched. You just didn't say no to Mr. Larkworthy. While we marched, we told Mr. Larkworthy who Parks was, and why we'd had a telescopic lens trained on him.

He just kept shaking his head. "I would think you would know better," he said to Pia, which sort of suggested that he thought Nick and I *didn't,* if you follow the thought to its logical conclusion. Which I think Nick did, because he suddenly got very quiet. I guess he'd figured out that after this little escapade, Mr. Larkworthy wouldn't be too keen on his taking out his little girl.

When we got to his building, Parks buzzed us up. When he opened the door, he had a phone in his hand. "Start talking, or I start dialing."

Pia the diplomat began brilliantly. She name-dropped. "Hello, Mr. McKenna. You know Annie and Nick, but I should introduce myself. I'm Pia Larkworthy, and this is my father, David Larkworthy."

A strange expression passed over Parks's face, as though he were a kid who'd been caught stealing candy by Michael Jordan. What I mean is, he looked guilty and thrilled at the same time.

"David Larkworthy, of Tine-Worthy Press?" he asked.

"The same," Mr. Larkworthy said.

"Mr. Larkworthy, what a pleasure," Parks said, pumping his hand. "I didn't know that you . . . what I mean is, I had no idea that . . ."

"Neither did I, Mr. McKenna," Mr. Larkworthy said. "I am not here to defend my daughter. I think she owes you an explanation."

"I'm sure no explanation is necessary," Parks said. All of a sudden, he was Mr. Congeniality.

"Oh, yes, it is." Mr. Larkworthy pushed Pia forward. "Explain," he said firmly.

"We're investigating the Key West murder," Pia said. "Not that we suspected you, Mr. McKenna. Not at all. But apparently the murder was committed by someone who was on the charter flight down to Key West, so we're just . . . examining all the possibilities."

Parks's face got very red. "So you're spying on me because you think I'm a murderer?"

"Not exactly," Pia said. "We were investigating. There's a difference."

"Well, I don't see it!" Parks said testily. "You invaded my privacy!" He seemed to remember that Mr. Larkworthy was there. With an effort, he tried to calm himself. "I can't believe I would be a suspect in a murder case. Why didn't you come and talk to me about it? I have an ironclad alibi. I was at Chip Waddell's taping."

Nick gave me a sidelong look. We knew that Parks had sneaked out of the taping. But it was probably better, at this point, not to let him know that we knew. He might dig himself in deeper.

"You could have left early," I said.

"I might have stepped out for five minutes or so," Parks blustered. "But I came back. I stayed until the very end, and I can prove it."

He stalked off toward the kitchen, and we followed. He snatched a jar off the shelf. "I got the pepper sauce Chip handed out. That means I was there at the end! This sauce isn't available in stores." He held up the jar of Waddell's Homemade Sin Hot Red Chili Sauce.

Nick drifted back toward the kitchen table. He flipped the cover down on the laptop.

"And how do you explain this?" he asked, pointing to the label. "This is Chip Waddell's laptop."

Parks just stood there, his mouth gaping open like a fish. Then he looked at Nick with real hatred.

"Perhaps you have an explanation," Mr.

Larkworthy said, crossing his arms. "I'd like to hear it myself."

"I found it," Parks said rapidly. "I just haven't told Chip yet."

"Until you stole his recipes?" Mr. Larkworthy inquired, glancing at the pad next to the computer.

"He stole from me first!" Parks cried. "His barbecue recipe, the one that made his fortune—that was in my family for generations. He stole it when we were in business together. Oh, he says he changed it—he uses maple syrup instead of brown sugar, and throws in another spice or two—but he got me to copy it out, and he stole it, all right. He deserves payback!"

"So you're stealing his recipes now?" Pia said. "Seems like you're both pretty sleazy."

"I'm changing them! Just like he changed mine," Parks said. "He's a big phony, with his down-home act. He grew up in Atlanta. He knows more about freeways than farms."

"You tried to steal Nick's bag at the airport," I said.

"I didn't!" Parks looked honestly dumbfounded. "I picked it up by mistake, I swear. Not only that, after I picked up *my* bag, it was stolen."

"Oh, come on," Nick said disgustedly. "Do you expect us to believe that?"

"I can prove that, too." Parks hurried into the other room. In only a minute he was back. He flourished a piece of paper in the air. "I filled out a report with the airline."

We all bent over the form.

"It looks legit," Nick said. "But we can always check it out."

"It still doesn't clear you," I said. "You could have pretended to have had your luggage stolen. You did steal that laptop. And you could have stolen Bob Summerhall's knives and committed the murder!"

Parks looked at us in disbelief. "Are you kids out to ruin my life, or what?"

"It's time we left Mr. McKenna alone," Mr. Larkworthy said. "It's been a long night."

"I'll say," Parks said. He trailed behind us to the front door. "I hope this won't affect your consideration of my proposal,

Mr. Larkworthy," he said desperately.

Mr. Larkworthy paused in the hallway. "Not at all, Mr. McKenna," he said in a dignified way. "Your proposal has already been rejected."

He closed the door softly on Parks's moan.

"It was red," Nick said excitedly. We'd left Pia and Mr. Larkworthy at the corner. By the look Pia's father had given Nick, I didn't think Nick would be sharing turkey with the family at Thanksgiving.

"Mr. Larkworthy's face? I'll say," I said. "I think you just got on his very own personal Least Likely to Succeed with Me list."

"The pepper sauce," Nick said. "It was red. But that sauce is already in the stores. Chip gave out jars of his Green Homemade Sin. Not red."

"You're right!" I exclaimed. "So Parks was definitely lying. I thought maybe I'd missed him coming back to the taping on the video. He could have been off-camera, I guess."

"Didn't Chip's laptop get stolen that

night?" Nick asked. "Maybe that's where it happened. That's why Parks left. He didn't find it—he stole it. You were right, Annie."

"I was just trying to scare Parks when I accused him," I said. "It's a big jump from stealing to murder."

"Yeah," Nick said. "But people make the leap all the time."

Nick and I figured we had a couple of days in the city to investigate on our own. We hadn't reckoned on the parental network. Mr. Larkworthy called Nick's mother, who called Joe. It was Doghouse City. Mom put her foot down and ordered me back to Scull Island, pronto.

So I ended up finishing the paint job in the nursery. As I swished the second coat on the walls, I had time to think. I guess I was kind of ashamed of myself. Pia wasn't an awful person. She had been nice to me no matter what dig I'd sent in her general direction. She'd seemed to really care about Nick. She wasn't a ditz, and she didn't throw her money in your face like some kids did. Nick could have done better, but he could have done worse. It was inevitable that he'd have a girlfriend, so I might as well accept Pia. Maybe Nick's Pia-worship would die down after they'd been together awhile. I looked forward to that.

As I painted, I noticed what a nice shade of yellow Joe had picked. It wasn't too bright, or too eggy, or too sickly looking. I'm not a big yellow fan. But the room felt better. Instead of a dark room where we stuck things we didn't want anymore, like old furniture and paperbacks all bent out of shape from summer days at the beach, it was bright and welcoming. Joe had painted an old dresser white, and Mom had about ten swatches of curtains sitting by the window. This weekend, they would pick out a carpet. It was like they were waiting for this really important guest. They were going out of their way to make sure the person would be comfortable.

That made me think of when Mom and I had moved in with Joe. He had consulted me about my room, and made sure that everything in it was chosen by me. He had gone out of his way to make me feel wanted. How could I complain if he gave his new child the same attention?

Nick was right. I hated that. I was acting like a brat. Sure, I felt left out of Mom and Joe's happiness. I was afraid Nick would feel closer to his blood sib than to me. But I could have those feelings still and act like a person.

Maybe I'd throw Mom a baby shower, I thought as I ran the roller down the wall. Maybe I'd even invite Pia. Well, then again, maybe not. How far did you have to go to be a good person?

The phone rang, and I snatched it up before Mom or Joe did, hoping it would be Nick. It always feels better to check in with another inmate of the parental house of shame.

"How's the domestic temperature with you?" Nick asked without even saying hello.

"Frosty," I said. "But I'm painting the nursery, so I'm hoping for a warming trend tonight."

"I've got a Siberian winter here," Nick said with a sigh. "I can't call Pia, because her dad decided I was a Bad Influence. You know, sometimes I think I'm just destined to be a screwup, no matter what."

Nick sounded truly bummed. "I have an idea," I said. "Why don't you come out here? Joe and Mom are thawing, I promise. And you can't see Pia, anyway."

"That's not a bad idea," Nick said, brightening. "If I hustle, I could catch the morning train and be in time for the three o'clock ferry."

"I'm sort of grounded, but I think Joe and Mom would let me meet the ferry," I said. "Hey, maybe you can still win Mr. Larkworthy over with those cigars. A present usually softens a parental situation."

"I left the cigars at your house," Nick said. "I can bring them back to the city when I go. Listen, I'm outta here. Just make sure you finish the paint job by the time I get there." With a mad chuckle, Nick signed off.

I hung up and went back to my roller. I would be glad of Nick's company. After all, a murderer was on the loose. It was probably better that I was sort-of grounded.

Still, it was spring out there, and I was stuck inside, inhaling paint fumes. The days were getting longer. Maybe Joe and Mom would relax the patrols a little and let Nick and I go to the beach tonight for the sunset. . . .

My roller stopped in midroll. I heard the *ping*. That's what I call it when a lightbulb goes off in my head, and I make a truly brilliant connection.

"The days are getting longer!" I announced to the yellow wall.

I had forgotten about daylight savings time. There had been a time change the day of the murder! Sure, mostly everyone had changed clocks and watches.

But what about that video camera?

It would explain everything. Why Chip had lied, for instance. He'd said the taping was over at eleven, when the timer had said it was only ten. But he hadn't lied. The timer was wrong!

I dropped the roller in the pan. That meant that *all* the times on the tape were wrong!

I ran to my room. Wally the technician

had given me a business card with his number on it, in case I had any more questions. Quickly, I punched out the number. I was put through to Editing Bay C.

"Wally, this is Annie Hanley, remember, the girl who came in to see the Chip Waddell tape?" There was a silence. "I ate all your French fries?" I added.

"Oh, right. How're you doin'?"

"Great. Listen, I have a question. The timer on the video camera—does it automatically change during daylight savings time, or does someone have to reset it?"

"Somebody has to reset it," Wally said. "But you don't have to worry about that. Nobody's going to ask you about a cam timer at an interview, kid. We're not that thorough."

"I know, but I'm, like, compulsive, so I like to go over everything," I said. "Take the Waddell tape from Key West, for example. What if the timing was off by an hour? The show ended at ten, but Chip said it ended at eleven."

"So somebody didn't reset the timer," Wally said. "It happens. Takes a couple days. It doesn't matter, I'm telling you. It's not a live show, so why do we care what time it is?"

But I do. "So nobody reset the timer on the Waddell show?" I persisted.

"If the timer said it ended at ten, they didn't," Wally said. "I happen to know that show ran late. Chip's shows always do. He doesn't know when to stop talking. Don't worry, kid. Nobody's gonna get fired, okay? You've got to learn to relax about life."

"You're absolutely right," I said. I thanked him and hung up. Then I ran to my notes. I spread them out on the bed and checked out the times.

Parks hadn't left at 8 P.M. He'd left at nine. So even though he'd lied about staying for the whole show, he had an ironclad alibi. He'd probably lied just to score points with Pia's dad, and to cover up the laptop theft.

I looked down at Marcia's times. Instead of leaving at 7:12 and returning at 7:36, she'd actually left at 8:12 and returned at 8:36. In other words, she'd had just enough time to murder Bradley Binks and get back to the taping before she was missed.

The Blue Iguana was near the water. Marcia even could have disposed of the hand on the way. I shuddered, thinking about it. But why had she—or whoever— cut off the hand in the first place? We still hadn't figured that out.

I picked up the phone and called Nick, but the answering machine was on. I knew he probably had left to catch the train, anyway. Just as I hung up, the phone rang again, and I picked it up.

"Annie? It's Pia," Pia said in a hurried voice. "I know Nick is on the way."

"Yeah," I said cautiously.

"I just wanted to let you guys know this," Pia said. "I plugged Bob Summerhall into my dad's super-search engine. And he's . . . not there. I looked up his journalism, his house deed, his office address, home address, unlisted phone number . . . nothing. Remember that column he was supposed to have written for that Italian magazine? I called their offices. They've never heard of him."

"Maybe they just didn't understand you," I said.

"I speak Italian, Annie. Believe me, this guy didn't write for them," Pia continued. "He's no Mediterranean Maestro. It's not just that he lied. It's that he doesn't exist. He's the invisible man."

"Do you think he's our guy?" I asked slowly. "He has an alibi."

"But what if he's involved, and he hired someone to do it?" Pia persisted. "Look, I don't know. I just want to warn you guys. Something smells extremely fishy. If I were you and I bumped into Bob Summerhall, I'd run the other way."

19//way deadly

My first inclination was to ignore everything that Pia had said. It seemed perfectly possible to me that she'd gotten everything all wrong. When it came to belief in her genius abilities, Nick was flying solo.

Besides, I was just gearing up to present Marcia Fallows as our number one suspect. Just because Pia had dug up way more dirt on Bob Summerhall didn't mean I wasn't ahead of her. I didn't have any fancy search engines, but I did have a brain. Of course, it hadn't been functioning at peak efficiency. I should have remembered about daylight savings time from the very beginning.

I wasn't exactly looking forward to informing Nick that I'd blown the timing of the murder scenario. And I especially wasn't looking forward to telling him that his dream girl had found out plenty on Bob Summerhall. I'd have to hear him sing her praises for five hours. So I decided to drop in on Chief Plutsky to see if anything new had turned up on the victim. At least I'd have some tidbit to offer besides my bungling of the timing.

Besides, I hadn't visited the chief in about a week, and he was probably missing me.

I wasn't bothered by the fact that he dropped his head in his hands when he saw me. I knew that was just a cover.

I threw myself into the chair across from him. "Come on, admit it. You're glad to see me."

"Why are you here?" he groaned. "And don't tell me you wanted to bring me doughnuts."

"My hands are empty," I said, spreading them out. "I haven't come to tempt you. Only to pump you for more info. Have you talked to the Key West police lately?"

Chief Plutsky blew out a breath. "Listen to me, Annie. I want you to drop this."

"I have dropped it," I said. "This is just idle curiosity."

For some reason, Chief Plutsky didn't believe me. "I'm dead serious," he said. "There's something going on here that makes me nervous. Something bigger than we think."

"Like what?" I asked, leaning forward.

He slammed his hand down on the desk, and I jumped. "That's what I mean!" he said. "Can't I just tell you that, and have you leave it alone? I'm protecting you, Annie. You're just a kid!"

It was a good thing Nick wasn't here. That "kid" reference would have sent him into orbit. "So if I'm a kid, I have to shut off my brain?" I asked. "Come on, Chief. I have a right to know. I found the body. And my family almost ended up in a minivan coffin, remember?"

He sighed. "I'll tell you what I know, which isn't much. The last piece of information I got out of Key West is that they found out this Binks guy had been in contact with someone in Tripoli. As in Libya. Then, all of a sudden, the pipeline dried up. I couldn't get word one out of those guys. Which means one thing to me."

"Cover-up?" I breathed.

The chief shook his head. "Feds. Once they step in, the local police are out of the loop."

"So some federal agency is investigating the murder," I said slowly. "Maybe because of the smuggling angle."

"Very smart," Chief Plutsky said. "And exactly my point. This guy had smuggled stuff like cigars for the black market, or cash for folks who don't want the Feds to know about it. But he must have moved on to the big time."

"What are you saying?" I breathed. "Terrorism?"

"I'm saying, keep your nose out of this," Chief Plutsky said evenly. "There are all kinds of bad stuff on the black market. Explosives, guns, chemical weapons, biological weapons, nuclear devices . . ."

I sat there, my mouth open. If the chief had meant to scare me, he'd done an awesome job.

"You see what I mean?" Chief Plutsky said softly. "It's a scary world out there, Annie. Stay safe."

@ @ @

Chief Plutsky had spooked me. No question. I hadn't counted on tangling with international terrorists. Even Nick would have to admit that this angle was out of our league.

He'd given me good advice, but he'd also set my mind going. And once that happens, you just can't stop because somebody tells you to. It's like thinking the word "yawn," and all of a sudden your mouth is open, and you're yawning all over the place.

If my geography was correct, Libya was on the Mediterranean. And Bob Summerhall had spent the winter in Tunisia. What if Summerhall and Binks were in cahoots somehow? They could have been involved in smuggling something way scary like weapons. If they'd had a falling out, Summerhall could have planned to kill Binks. Maybe he'd lied about his knives being stolen. Maybe he'd given them to the hit man he'd hired. Or maybe he'd done the deed himself. I'd asked Joe twice if he was sure about Summerhall being at his demo, but maybe

Summerhall had reset Joe's watch. Or maybe Joe had forgotten about daylight savings time.

I wanted to grill Joe again, but it was time to meet Nick at the ferry. I walked over and sat on one of the benches, watching as the ferry chugged toward the dock. I couldn't wait to see Nick. Maybe he could figure out something that we'd overlooked.

The ferry bumped gently against the dock. The workers buzzed around the lines, tying it up. First, the people on foot got off. I spotted Nick right away, striding down the gangway in jeans and a T-shirt, his bulky backpack slung over one shoulder. He was with someone, I saw. Someone compact and muscular, with a receding hairline. . . .

Nick was with Bob Summerhall.

20//baa, baa black sheep

I stood up in a panic. Nick waved. I ran toward him. I grabbed his arm.

"Remember Mr. Summerhall?" Nick asked me. "I bumped into him on the ferry—"

Bob Summerhall opened his mouth to greet me, but I jumped in first. "Howdoyoudo," I said in a rush. "Nick, you have to come with me."

"What's the matter?" Nick's face suddenly went pale. "Is it your mom?"

"No . . ." I said. Why hadn't I noticed Bob Summerhall's beady eyes? "But it is, uh, a family emergency. Will you excuse us, Mr. Summerhall?"

"Sure, kids—" Bob Summerhall began as I yanked Nick away.

"What is it?" Nick asked tensely as soon

as we were out of earshot. "What happened?"

"It's Bob Summerhall," I said. "He could be our guy!"

Nick dropped his backpack. His face flushed. "This is about the *case?* You scared me to death. I thought someone was in the hospital, Annie!"

"I'm sorry, Nick," I said. "I really am. But I had to get you away from Bob Summerhall! You *should* be scared to death." Quickly, I filled him in on what Pia had told me, and what I'd learned at the police station.

"This does sound scary," Nick admitted once I'd finished. "I didn't figure on terrorists. Come on, let's sit down for a minute."

We plopped down on a bench. People were still driving off the ferry. Other cars pulled up to meet passengers. Dogs bounded off the ferry, and kids were pushed in strollers. Bob Summerhall had disappeared. We were safe here.

"If you think about it, Scull Island is a good place for terrorist operations," I said. "If they have a boat, they can be on the open sea in minutes. And there are some houses that are pretty isolated."

Nick nodded. "I see what you're saying, Annie. But let's slow down. First of all, I don't think Joe would screw up on the time. I don't think Summerhall killed Bradley Binks. Marcia Fallows made up things about her past, too. Maybe Summerhall made up his résumé so that he could get a gig at the Food Festival. That's why he picked Tunisia—your average editor wouldn't check those references. It's too hard."

"Okay, what about Parks?" I said. "He could have been in on it. Remember when you followed him to that lab?"

"He was having Chip's pepper sauce analyzed," Nick said. "I went back and bribed the guy with some of Joe's old jazz LPs. I gave him two Paul Desmonds and a Charlie Parker for the info. By the way, don't tell my dad."

"Oh," I said, deflated.

"Parks is just what he looks like," Nick said. "A lowlife trying to get a book deal. And you told me he has an alibi after all, remember? The timing on the videotape?"

"Now I'm getting confused," I grumbled.

"Okay, let's go over the clues one more time," Nick said. "The trick in an investigation isn't so much gathering clues as deciding which are important. Maybe we've missed some connection that's right in front of us. Our suspects seem to have alibis, first of all."

"Except for Marcia," I pointed out.

"Right," Nick said. "But any one of them could have been working with someone we don't know. Especially if we're dealing with arms smuggling. There could be a whole ring of people. Our guy—or girl—has a cover as a chef, or a journalist. That allows them the freedom to go to other countries without arousing suspicion. But who isn't who they say they are?"

"Just about everybody, it seems," I said gloomily.

Nick continued: "Okay. Parks McKenna. He stole a laptop. Lied about being at the taping until the end. Took a sauce sample to be analyzed. That doesn't add up to weapons smuggling somehow. I mean, he did own a restaurant. How did he get into terrorism? It just doesn't fit."

"It doesn't fit with Chip, either," I said. "I mean, I can see him smuggling Cuban cigars for his restaurant. But he's got a great career going. He's not a terrorist."

"What else do we have?" Nick said. "The stolen laptop we can account for."

"What about your duffel?" I asked. "Something's weird there. Maybe Parks wasn't lying when he said he picked it up by mistake. But why was *his* stolen?"

"Wait a second," Nick breathed. "Maybe someone saw Parks pick up my duffel. But they didn't see me take it back again. So when they took his duffel—"

"They thought it was yours!" I said. "That makes perfect sense. But why would someone try to steal your duffel?"

Nick shrugged. "They knew we saw the murder. They knew they wanted to scare us, but they still hadn't figured out how, exactly. Maybe they were hoping my house keys were in the duffel. They could break into the house."

"And when they didn't get your duffel, they had to try to scare us, or kill us, on the ferry," I said. "But who could it have been?"

"If Chip and Parks arc out, that leaves us with Bob Summerhall and Marcia Fallows," Nick concluded.

"Summerhall has an alibi," I said. "But he's a man without a past."

"Marcia doesn't have an alibi," Nick said. "But she *is* a real journalist." He reached into his backpack and took out a sheaf of papers. "Here's the printout of all her articles. Sure, she may have exaggerated how much she knows about cooking. But at least she has a past that's legit, right?"

The ferry had finished loading for the return trip. I heard the blast of the horn and watched it slowly reverse out of the slip. I thought back on meeting Marcia and Dr. Dick on the ferry that day. If only I'd had a chance to ask her more questions. If only that kid hadn't dropped that snow globe—

"Nick!" I exclaimed. "On the ferry, Marcia completely took over when a kid cut himself on this glass snow globe he dropped."

Nick nodded. "You told me. You said anybody that nice couldn't be a murderer."

"It wasn't that she was *nice*," I said, thinking back. "She was smooth. I was thinking professional mom, but what if she was a real pro? Do you think she could have had some kind of medical training?"

"Well, she did get a job as a science reporter," Nick said. He ran his finger down the page. "Maybe we could look up some of these articles. Maybe she trained in medicine, then went into journalism. You never know. Are you thinking about the hand?"

"Exactly," I said, nodding. "The police said it had been almost surgically severed. We kept thinking that a chef did it. But who better than a doctor, or a nurse?"

"True," Nick said. He scanned the titles of the articles. "'New Hope for Osteoporosis.' 'Fiber That Fights Cancer.' 'Loose Cannons Haunt Bioweapons Conference.' 'New FDA Guidelines Stump Experts.' 'Vitamin E: New Studies . . .'"

"Fascinating stuff," I said. "I'm looking forward to reading them." I gazed out to sea. The Scull Island ferry chugged off toward New London. Behind it, I saw a smaller ferry heading east. It was the

Blackberry Island ferry, which was smaller. It didn't take any paying passengers. You had to work on Blackberry Island to board it. Something nagged at my brain. It wasn't a ping. Not yet. It was more like a . . . pong. *Pong, pong, pong . . .*

"Wait a second," Nick said. "We're forgetting something totally important. The cigars! I took those cigars from Bradley Binks, Annie! And *I never opened the box!*"

I was listening to Nick, but I was also listening to the *pong* in my head. What was it that Dr. Dick worked on? Sheep, I remembered. He worked on sheep diseases. "Nick, what is that disease that sheep get?" I asked. "We studied it in biology."

"Annie, are you listening to me?" Nick asked excitedly. "What if something is in that box!"

"Louis Pasteur found the vaccine," I said. "I remember from class. We saw a documentary on it."

"Annie!" Nick cried, frustrated. "I'm telling you that whatever was being smuggled could be in—"

"Anthrax!" I cried, interrupting him. "It's in—"

"The cigar box," we said together.

For a moment, we just stared at each other.

"Could it be true?" I breathed.

Nick looked back down at the papers in his lap. He ran a finger down the titles again. "Biological weapons," he read slowly. "Marcia wrote an article on it. Anthrax is a biological weapon, Annie. And I don't think it takes very much of it to infect a whole lot of people."

"And Dr. Dick works on Blackberry Island, where they study anthrax," I said.

Suddenly, I noticed that the parking lot was deserted. The next ferry wasn't due for another hour and a half. The silence was eerie.

"We'd better go to Chief Plutsky," I said nervously. Behind Nick, a black Jeep Cherokee pulled into the parking lot. The person must have gotten the ferry times wrong.

"We don't have enough," Nick argued. "He'll throw us out of his office."

"Nick, it doesn't matter," I said. "What if

anthrax is in that box? We can't handle it. I mean, literally. I'm not even sure what form it's in. What if there's a test tube or something in that box? What if it got loose?" I gripped Nick's arm. "Nick, the baby— Mom is home. What if she cleans your room . . ."

"You sold me," Nick said, standing up. "Let's move."

The Cherokee pulled up in front of us. Probably a tourist asking about ferry times. You'd think they would make a phone call.

Then the door popped open. Marcia Fallows was at the wheel. Dr. Dick was in the passenger seat.

"Hey kids!" Marcia called. "Want a ride?"

I nudged Nick. "That's okay," I said. "We want to walk."

"I think we'd better take the ride, Annie," Nick said. His voice sounded strange.

"What are you talking about?" I whispered.

Nick pointed with his chin toward Marcia. That was when I noticed the gun.

21//bioterror

Call me slow on the uptake. I have no excuse. I must even point out that I have been in this position before. Nick and I were held at gunpoint by Sal the pizza killer. But that doesn't mean I'm experienced. My brain fizzed and popped in a blank sort of way. I forgot how to move my feet.

Nick grabbed my arm and squeezed it. That meant *hang in there*.

"I won't hurt you if you cooperate," Marcia said. She was wearing sunglasses, so I couldn't see her eyes. Her voice sounded completely casual, but the gun wasn't so casual. "Your cooperation is essential."

You just don't argue with a gun. We climbed into the backseat of the Jeep. As soon as we were inside, Marcia clicked the automatic door locks.

Marcia made a left at the parking lot entrance. That meant she was heading away from town, toward the less populated end of the island. This was not the greatest news.

"Hold the gun, Dick," she said. "I have to drive."

"I don't want to hold that thing," Dick said.

"Grow a backbone!" Marcia snapped. "Do I have to do everything?"

Dr. Dick took the gun gingerly. "Don't move," he said, training it on us. He didn't seem thrilled to be holding the gun. This could be good news or bad news, depending on how you looked at it. Chances were that he'd be reluctant to shoot us. But there was a good chance he'd get so nervous, he'd shoot us by mistake. Who would want to deal with those odds? So Nick and I didn't move.

"So where is it?" Marcia asked.

"Where's what?" Nick asked.

"Don't play games with me, kid," Marcia snapped.

"Don't call me kid, lady," Nick said.

"Kid's got a mouth on him," Marcia

said. She took off her dark glasses and looked at Nick in the rearview mirror. "Look, Mouth, I just want to recover my property, okay? Then I'll let you go. You grabbed it from my associate, and we want it back."

"Why should I help you out?" Nick asked.

"Let's review," Marcia said. "I have the gun. How's that for a reason?"

"We're not going to negotiate with armed terrorists," I said.

Marcia's mouth twisted. "Who are you, the president? And don't call me a terrorist. I'm a supplier."

"That's just what drug dealers say," I said. "Then people end up dead."

"Now she's comparing me to some sleazy drug dealer," Marcia said to Dr. Dick. "Did you hear that?"

"My hearing is fine," Dr. Dick said.

"Just what do you want from us?" Nick asked defiantly.

"I want the box," Marcia said. "I've got a very important meeting to attend, and I can't go without it. Understand?"

"I don't get it, Marcia," Nick said. "You're a legitimate journalist. How did you get mixed up with a bunch of terrorists?"

"Hey, I'm a legitimate scientist," Dr. Dick spoke up, twitching his nose. "I'm not a criminal!"

"Then what are you doing selling anthrax?" I asked.

"She made me do it," Dr. Dick said sulkily.

"Wimp," Marcia snarled, taking a corner practically on two wheels. "Look, not that it's any of your business, but I didn't start out selling the stuff. I did an article on bioweapons, and I met Dr. Suave here. Do you kids know what happened when the Soviet Union fell? They had a secret plant with top scientists developing biological weapons. Anthrax, smallpox, Ebola—you name it, they studied it, used genetic engineering to make it more toxic, even combined different viruses to make them more deadly. Then they found out a way to pack it into a missile."

"We have a treaty against biological weapons, don't we?" Nick asked.

Marcia snorted. "Sure. The problem is that when the program was shut down, some of the scientists disappeared. Nobody knew where. And nobody is quite sure what they took when they left. How hard could it be to tuck some samples into your pockets that you could sell to the right people? That research is worth billions to certain governments."

"That's scary," I said.

"You bet, sweetie," Marcia said. "So I ask Dr. Dick here about it. And he hems and haws, but practically admits we haven't done enough to prepare. I ask about security where he works, and he hems and haws again. If you wanted to steal it, I said, could you? That's when I came up with my idea. Why doesn't he steal some anthrax just as an experiment? All he has to do is slip it into his pocket, get on the ferry. No one would be the wiser. Then I'd write an exposé. I'd win the Pulitzer prize!"

"Or go to jail," I pointed out.

"No jury would convict me," Marcia said.

"So what happened?" Nick asked. "How did you wind up trying to sell it?"

"Once I had it, I got to thinking," Marcia said. "I mean, there's anthrax out there. What's a little vial of it? But the right people could pay me enough to set me up for life. And nobody would be the wiser. Especially if Dr. Dick did a little more genetic engineering. Mixed it with smallpox, say."

"I didn't want to do it," Dr. Dick said.

"Yeah, but you just love making that measly salary and waiting for retirement, right?" Marcia sneered. "So I contacted someone I know. From a past life, you might say."

"Bradley Binks," Nick said.

Marcia looked surprised. "Yeah, my ex-husband. Not the most honest person in the world. He operated a smuggling business down in Florida. Small-time stuff, but I figured he knew the right people. I didn't figure he'd want a fifty percent cut. I should have known. The guy is a louse. I supported him for years back when I was a nurse—"

"You were a nurse!" I looked at Nick triumphantly.

"A surgical nurse. I worked like a dog," Marcia said. "Double shifts. All Brad did was gamble our money away. Who knew a crook would come in so handy."

"So you decided to meet in Key West," Nick said. "You'd contact him at the Web site. And he'd contact the buyers the same way."

"You kids messed everything up," Marcia said furiously. "Brad thought you were the buyers. Then he saw you were kids, and said no deal. But you went ahead and grabbed the box."

"I'm a New Yorker," Nick said. "I get mad."

"Brad was too embarrassed to tell me he'd lost the stuff to a couple of kids. So I guess he followed you and tried to break into your rooms, but I didn't figure that out until later. Parks blabbed to me about finding you two with a box of cigars. But I didn't know that then. Brad just kept stalling me. So I figured he'd double-crossed me," Marcia said.

"So you stole Bob Summerhall's knives. And you stabbed Brad," Nick said.

"I was pretty angry," Marcia said, as though she'd slashed his tires, not killed him in cold blood. "Then after he was lying there, I noticed he still wore his wedding ring. It matches mine. I thought somebody might have noticed my ring." I looked at Marcia's right hand, at the thick gold ring with the distinctive scrollwork.

"Why didn't you just cut off his finger?" Nick asked with a shiver.

"I also thought it would slow up the police if Brad didn't have fingerprints," Marcia said. "I was going for the other hand when you kids showed up."

"You were still there?" I asked.

"I didn't have much time," Marcia said. "I had to get back to Chip's taping. That was my alibi."

"So you're a thief and a murderer and a terrorist," Nick said. "What an impressive résumé."

Marcia suddenly swerved over to the shoulder of the road. She turned around. Her eyes glinted fiercely at us. "It's all your fault I killed Brad!" Marcia suddenly yelled. "I'm not guilty! You are! Both of you. I thought he'd double-crossed me, and he hadn't. You made me do it!"

We stared at Marcia. I was beginning to realize she was seriously nuts.

"Now I'm in a mess with the people he contacted, and that's your fault, too," Marcia went on. "I have to get them that anthrax!" She grabbed the gun from Dr. Dick. "Tell me where it is. Now. I know you have it, Mouth. And I know you live here and in the city. So either we drive to the city, or we drive to your house now. And if you lie to me, somebody gets hurt."

Nick crossed his arms. He stared at her stonily.

Slowly, Marcia pointed the gun at me.

Nick uncrossed his arms. "It's here," he said. "On Scull Island. In my room."

"That's better." Marcia gave the gun back to Dr. Dick. She peeled out onto the road and headed back toward town.

"We're going to do this nice and easy," she said. "Act nice, and your family lives. Try something stupid, and everybody dies."

22//frantic

Marcia told us what to say. She was renovating her house. She wanted to see the
upstairs. If Joe or Kate tried to show her, we
would discourage them. Then, in Nick's
room, she would see the box of cigars and
Nick would offer them to her, if Kate or Joe
were close by, listening.

We drove up and parked in front. Across
the street, the Marshall house was being
renovated. They had moved back to
Cleveland, and the new owners needed
more space. I glanced at the hefty workmen
as we walked to our door, wishing I could
scream, *Help!* They could take Marcia, for
sure.

But nothing happened. The sun continued to shine, and the grass continued to
grow, and we opened our front door and let

a madwoman capable of infecting thousands of people inside our house.

Nick and I stood in the hall for a minute. We heard the sound of someone in the kitchen and we knew it was Joe, working on his new cookbook. Should we head directly upstairs, or involve Joe? Maybe it would be better to get Marcia in and out as quickly as possible. But if we let her leave, all those deaths would be on our hands. I glanced at Nick. His gaze was just as bleak and desperate as mine must have been.

"This has to look as normal as possible," Marcia said between her teeth.

"Let's go upstairs," Nick said.

"What about Joe?" Marcia asked.

"He won't know we're here if we're quiet," Nick said. I knew he was trying not to involve Joe. But suddenly, I had an idea.

"He might get suspicious," I said. Nick glowered at me. "We always say hello when we come home."

"Okay," Marcia said grimly. "Let's go say hello to Dad."

We walked into the kitchen. Joe was stirring something at the stove. He looked startled to see Marcia and Dr. Dick.

"Hello, Marcia," he said. "Hi, uh—"

"Dick," Marcia supplied pleasantly. "That smells marvelous, Joe."

"Just a little marinara," Joe said.

"I bumped into your kids at the ferry," Marcia explained, "and they graciously said I could peek at your upstairs. I'm renovating, and believe me, it's been a process."

"Let me show you," Joe said, beginning to take off his chef's apron.

"I wouldn't dream of bothering you," Marcia said quickly.

"Really, Joe," I said. "You stay here. We'll just be a second. I told Marcia that you found the perfect shade of yellow for the nursery, and she's dying to take a peek."

Marcia looked confused. She hadn't known that Mom was pregnant. But she recovered quickly. "I'm thinking of painting the sunroom yellow."

"Kate's napping in the family room, so stick to upstairs, okay?" Joe asked. He put the metal spoon back in the pan and began to stir.

"No problemo," Nick said.

I backed up against the table, where Joe's notes were spread out. Marcia grabbed me by the arm. "Let's go, Annie," she said pleasantly. Her cold hand squeezed my arm hard.

We all walked back toward the stairs. Nick took the lead. I followed, and then Marcia and Dr. Dick.

"Nick is upset because the new baby is taking over his room," I said. "He'll have to sleep downstairs once it comes."

Nick hesitated on the stairs for just a fraction. Then he kept going. He threw me a puzzled look over his shoulder.

"But he gets to sleep in the nursery for five whole months," I said. "It's completely redone."

Nick hit the hallway at the top. I held my breath. His room was to the right. The nursery was to the left. *Go left!* I screamed in my head. *Go left, Nick!* My plan wouldn't work if he didn't. It was our last hope.

Nick went left. The nursery door was open, and he went inside. I followed, with Marcia and Dick on my heels.

The dresser was covered in a sheet, and

there was no other furniture in the room. It smelled like wet paint. I moved to the corner, where the baby monitor sat on top of a small wooden table Joe was planning to refinish. With my back to Marcia, I turned it on. I had already turned on the one in the kitchen before Marcia had yanked me away.

"Where's the bed?" Marcia asked. "Where are all your belongings? This isn't your room!"

"I guess Joe moved your stuff out already," I said quickly. "Listen, Marcia, if you want to get your hands on that anthrax, you have to trust us."

"Trust you? Why should I trust you?" Marcia said. She rubbed the bridge of her nose. "Where's that cigar box? No more games, kids."

"How did you hide the anthrax?" I asked. The best I could do was stall. I prayed that Joe was listening and would pick up the phone and call Chief Plutsky.

"It's in a cigar tube," Marcia said. "You don't need much to wipe out a city, I guess."

"So you would let some terrorists release it on a New York City subway, or on a street?" Nick demanded. He didn't know what I was up to, but he was stalling, too.

"That's not my concern," Marcia said. "If they don't get it from me, they'll get it from somewhere else. Stop stalling! Let's go." She brandished the gun.

"You can put down the gun," I said. I knew Marcia wouldn't, but just in case Joe was listening, I wanted him to know she was armed.

We had no choice. We headed down the hall to Nick's room. The cigar box was sitting on his dresser. He handed it to Marcia. There was no sign of Joe, and I didn't hear a siren, or the sound of a car. But Chief Plutsky could be outside right now, if Joe acted quickly enough.

"Now you can go," Nick said.

"Come on," Marcia said, motioning with the gun.

"You said you'd let us go!" I protested.

"Did I say that?" Marcia asked Dr. Dick. She shook her head. "I didn't say that. I said nobody would get hurt if you cooperated. If I left you here, you'd call the police in about two seconds."

"Like Chief Plutsky would be any help," Nick scoffed. "Come on, Marcia. You're home free, and you know it."

"Not yet, Mouth," Marcia said evenly. "You're coming with me to the meeting. Only when I'm on a plane with my Swiss bank account numbers in hand do you go free. Dick will hold you until I'm clear."

Dick looked startled. "What do you mean, Dick will hold them? I'm not staying behind!"

Marcia turned the gun on Dick. "You'll do what I say. Enough arguing! Let's move out."

We started down the stairs again. Joe was still whistling in the kitchen. He probably hadn't heard anything at all! And now we were heading toward a meeting with international terrorists. Despite what Marcia had said, she could decide that we were a liability. Or the terrorists could. They'd never let us go. We were walking straight toward death.

23//a good strong wind

We didn't say good-bye to Joe. I felt tears knot my throat. Would I ever see him and Mom again? Nick slipped his hand into mine and squeezed it. His fingers felt comforting, but I knew he felt desperate, too.

We started down the walk toward the Jeep.

"Nice and slow," Marcia said through her smile, in case someone was watching. A workman was digging in the front yard across the street. I gazed at him helplessly, but he didn't look up.

Just then, I saw someone heading down the road toward us. It was Bob Summerhall!

"So we meet again!" he cried cheerfully. "A Key West reunion, right here on Scull Island!"

Marcia put a frozen smile on her face.

"Hi, Bob. I'd love to catch up, but we don't want to miss the ferry."

Bob looked at his watch. "Oh, it docsn't leave for another half hour. You have time." As he spoke, he kept walking. There was something purposeful in his eyes. He was moving swiftly and silently as a cat. Nick squeezed my hand. This time, it wasn't for comfort. It was a warning. *Be ready for anything!*

Marcia stiffened. She tried to nudge us forward. "Come on, kids. Get into the car."

But instead, Nick gave me a sudden shove, and I fell to one side. He leaped to the other. Bob Summerhall sprang forward, his stocky, muscular body suddenly purposeful and strong. He knocked Marcia flat!

It all happened so fast. The gun flew out of her fingers and landed a few inches away on the grass. The crew across the street raced toward us. One of them grabbed the gun. The others stood between Nick and me and Marcia. And Bob Summerhall held the cigar box.

There was only one problem. In the

scuffle, the box had opened. And Marcia held the anthrax.

She lay on her back. She had to. One of the workmen held a gun on her.

"FBI," he said. "You're under arrest for—"

"Don't bother," Marcia said. Her voice was a little breathless. She held up the anthrax. "You let me go, or I shake this tube." I saw that her thumb was over the top of the tube. She'd already opened it. "If you shoot me, the anthrax will be released. It's been genetically engineered with the smallpox virus. And there's a good strong wind today. I bet it makes it all the way to the mainland. Scull Island and half of Connecticut will be history."

The FBI agent was expressionless. Bob Summerhall tossed the cigar box on the grass. "Read her her rights," he said. "This has got to be by the book."

"Did you hear me?" Marcia screamed. She shook the anthrax, her thumb still firmly over the opening. "I'll let this go! I swear!"

Suddenly, Dr. Dick stepped forward. He

plucked the cigar tube from Marcia's hand. He shook it. I gasped as a fine brown cloud flew from the tube. It was caught by the wind and rode the current of air straight toward Main Street.

Dr. Dick leaned forward. "Sorry, Marcia. Even a wimp can pull a double cross. Because the joke's on you."

24//cincinnati chili

Exactly two weeks later, Joe cooked up a big pot of chili and served it over spaghetti, Cincinnati style. He made a huge green salad and garlic bread. It looked like way too much food, but these days, Mom was eating for two.

Plus, we had a weekend guest.

"Now, tell me all the background stuff I missed," Pia said as she helped herself to more grated cheddar cheese. It was amazing how much the Stick could pack away. She shot a look at Nick. "Nick filled me in on some details, but I bet he's way too modest."

I snorted, but Nick grinned and took a mock bow. "Aw, shucks. 'Twasn't nothin', ma'am."

"Sure," Pia said. "You and Annie bring down a major bioweapons smuggler. She holds you at gunpoint, threatens your family, and you don't even break a sweat. You two are major heroes."

"Which is why your dad finally let me see you again," Nick said. "That's the best thing that happened."

"Oh, yeah," I said. "The fact that half the population of Manhattan wasn't wiped out in a slow, lingering death is immaterial. You get to *date*."

To my surprise, Pia burst out laughing. She choked on her chili and had to drink an entire glass of water. When she finished, she started to laugh again. She had this seriously weird laugh that bubbled up and down the scale and every so often honked like a ferry horn. It made Nick laugh, and then Mom, and Joe. Then I started, too.

Finally, we stopped, because we were just about out of breath.

"You can never underestimate the self-absorption of a teenager," Pia said. "That's what my dad says, anyway." Grinning, she took another huge helping of chili. I was actually starting to like her. "So when did Dr. Dick go to the Feds?" she asked.

"Right after Marcia pitched him the scheme," I said. "He thought she was unbalanced."

"A dead-on diagnosis," Joe said.

"He looked like one of his sheep, but Dick was brave," Mom pointed out. "He went undercover, and Marcia could have found him out at any time."

"Not to mention that he actually had to spend time with her," Nick added.

"So he substituted a fake version of anthrax for the real thing," I said. "The Feds were waiting until the deal went down, so they could catch everybody."

"Until we screwed up the plan," Nick said. "They started to realize we were investigating the murder, but by then, it was too late."

"Bob Summerhall came to Scull Island to warn us," Joe said. "They were even considering moving us to a safe house. Instead, they replaced the renovation workers across the street with their guys. He took Kate to the police station to be safe."

"I didn't want to," Mom said. "They forced me."

"We had to think about the baby, too," Joe said. "But if I'd left, it would have looked too suspicious."

"But I knew something was wrong," Nick said. "You were using a metal spoon to stir your marinara."

Joe grinned. "I was?"

"I didn't notice," I said. "Well, I didn't register it. That was good thinking, Nick."

Pia looked from me to Nick. "What are you guys talking about?"

"Tomatoes are reactive with metal," Nick explained. "A chef is fussy about things like that. You don't want a metallic taste to your sauce. So Joe always uses a wooden spoon when he makes tomato sauce."

"Except when I'm scared out of my wits," Joe admitted with a grin. "I never expected Marcia to turn up at the house. Especially with my kids. And Bob had left with Kate. I didn't know what to do. I didn't know if the kids knew what Marcia was up to. That is, until Annie turned on the baby monitor. Then I realized that the Feds had to move right then. They couldn't wait. So I called Bob and alerted him that they would all be leaving. I was ready to take down Marcia myself if Bob didn't show up in time."

Mom covered Joe's hand with hers. "I'm glad you didn't."

"At least Marcia cooperated," Nick said. "She led the Feds to the meeting, and even wore a wire. They captured all the buyers of the anthrax."

"This story is so totally scary," Pia said. "It sounds like a book my dad would publish. I can't believe how brave this family is." She lifted her soda glass. "Here's to the Hanley-Annunciatos."

"Wait a sec," I said. "You were brave, too, Pia. You stood up to Parks McKenna and Chip Waddell—"

"Sure, a couple of cooks," Pia said. "Not exactly armed terrorists."

"But you didn't know that," I said. "You knew they could have been murderers. I say we make a toast to Pia, too. She pitched right in and was as brave—"

"And foolish," Mom put in.

"As the rest of us," I finished. "She's an honorary member of the Hanley-Annunciato clan."

Pia blushed as we all raised our glasses to her. I had already invited her to the baby shower I was throwing for Mom. She'd promised to help pick the decorations and the food, so at least the party would have some class. I didn't think Pia was going to be my best friend or anything, but she was a fact of life. Just like the baby was. I had a feeling the two of them would grow on me.

"All's well that ends well, I guess," Mom said. She patted her rounded belly. "But I could do with some peace and quiet until the baby comes."

"You'll get it," Joe told her. "Annie and Nick promised to be on their best behavior. Do I need to remind you that if Nick had come clean about the cigars, some of this could have been avoided? If Bob Summerhall had known that you'd taken that box from Binks, he would have stepped in sooner."

"You don't need to remind us," Nick mumbled. We'd already had serious lectures from Bob Summerhall, Chief Plutsky, and Joe and Mom. You can take a wild guess as to which one stung the most. Parents win out over law enforcement, every time. At least ours did.

"So no more investigations," Joe said. "Right, guys?"

"Absatively posalutely," I agreed. "Our detecting days are over."

Joe stood up to clear the dishes. "Let me help," Pia said, springing up. She brought plates to the sink with Joe, and Mom got up to get the dessert.

Nick turned to me. "That reminds me. Chief Plutsky told me about this strange murder case in Rhode Island," he told me in a low tone. "The Providence police are totally stumped."

"Why are you telling me this?" I asked uneasily.

Nick shrugged. "No reason."

I stood and picked up my plate. "Good."

"But I just want to point out one thing," Nick said. "After you get off the ferry, Rhode Island is only twenty minutes away. . . ."

danger.com

@9//Shiver/

by
jordan.cray

Okay. Here's the situation. I'm going to be totally upfront with you, except in the places where I might lie a little to make myself look better. What can I say? I'm an actor. You think Al Pacino is really five foot nine?

Say you're chatting online with a group of buddies for about a year. Say you develop a crush on one of the girls. Say the crush is of the major, heartbreaking variety. Say in order to impress said girl, you perhaps exaggerate your good qualities, maybe even make a few of them up. Then say said girl says: Let's meet!

You see my problem.

I pinned the printout of the e-mail to the bulletin board in my room. When I have a tough call, I like to make face with it. It makes me feel macho and decisive.

If only I wasn't so nervous. If only I knew what to do.

I had formed the chat group with four of my buddies from drama camp last summer. Dudley Firth, Ethan Viner, Wilson MacDougal, and I had become friends when we realized that we were the best actors at camp. Sure, there were other guys who thought the same thing. The difference was, we were right.

You might imagine that drama camp in the Berkshire Mountains of Massachusetts would be a great place to meet girls, and you'd be right. But except for Ethan, we all were big strikeouts in the babe department. When it came to confidence, we had it onstage. *Offstage,* we tended to turn into overcooked linguine in the presence of the opposite sex. Or else we'd hang around in a clump, telling bad jokes and insulting each other while laughing really loudly, so the girls would think we were having such a good time that we didn't need them at all.

Do girls see through that one? Don't tell me. Let me have my illusions.

Do you have any idea what it's like to be

surrounded by actresses and never get up the courage to snag a date? So at the end of August, we had a brainstorm. The camp newsletter listed everyone's e-mail address, and we wrote to the cutest girls and some of the cooler guys, inviting them to join an online chat group that would focus on theater.

Great idea, right? Well, sort of. The problem was word of mouth. Our idea mushroomed until we had to split into a whole bunch of chat rooms. Some idiot suggested that we divide by area, so I ended up in New England, since I go to boarding school in Massachusetts. Wilson, Ethan, and Dud live in New England, too, so they were in my group. In other words, we created a giant room to meet girls, and ended up talking to each other in the corner. Typical guy behavior, right?

The New England group thinned out gradually, until it was down to fifteen. Maybe people dropped out because Wilson can be obnoxious, or because Dudley can write LOL (which means laugh out loud, just in case you're not a Netizen) instead of an intelligent response until you're ready to scream. But two girls, TygrrEyz and Monarch99, hung in there. Other kids would drop in from time to time, but mostly it was just the six of us.

Soon, the core group of The Six was established. You had to be quick to keep up with us. You had to know theater and movies. You had to know who was great, and who was overrated, and who was up-and-coming. You had to be a star in your drama department. You had to be dedicated. You had to be serious.

We sent each other voice tracks of our monologues. We even applied to the same drama seminar over spring break. One of the highlights of the seminar is a Master Class with Trey Havel, who is just about the most famous acting coach around. He teaches at Julliard, where we all want to go next year.

The amazing thing was that we all got in. Except for Monarch, who decided not to apply at the last minute. She said her roommate invited her to go skiing in Aspen, and she'd be stupid to refuse. Her roommate's father is a big Broadway producer. "You infiltrate the system your way, and I'll do it my way," she wrote online. "We'll see who makes it big first."

I stared at the e-mail while I studied. I thought about it as I brushed my teeth. I made a decision lying in bed at night, and then reversed it in the morning. I thought about every exaggeration, every lie I'd told TygrrEyz.

For example, I hadn't played one of the leads in *The Glass Menagerie*. I worked the lights. I went to a boy's boarding school, and everybody has to pitch in. Besides, I wasn't the leading man type, like Ethan. I'm more of a character actor. You know, the actor who plays the leading man's best friend, or the moody son with a deep, dark, secret. I just don't have the chin or the cheekbones to play the lead. Scott Davis gets the lead in almost every production at my school. He has the cheekbones, and he's six feet tall.

As a matter of fact, there was one particular deep, dark secret I wasn't sharing with the group. My biggest success that year had been in *A Midsummer Night's Dream*.

What's the problem? Shakespeare is heavy stuff, right? I should be proud.

Here's the problem: I played Titania, Queen of the Fairies. As I mentioned, I go to an all-boys school. Occasionally, we do a production without any girls from neighboring boarding schools. My performance as Titania got a rave, but I decided to deep six that particular review.

TygrrEyz would take one look at me and know I'd lied. I wasn't a studly specimen. No director would cast me as the romantic lead. I was strictly a Titania kind of guy.

So why was I so hung up on impressing her? Let me tell you why. TygrrEyz was just about the smartest, funniest girl I'd ever not met.

"You're seriously stupid, guy," my roommate Mark told me. "All the girls you meet online are potential gila monsters."

But TygrrEyz couldn't be. First of all, she usually gets the lead in her school productions. Only babes get the lead in school productions. She also has a completely sexy voice. She sent me her audition tape for the seminar, and I nearly swallowed the tape recorder. I hung over it, listening to every husky word.

But what I really like about Tiger is that she gets me, and I get her. It's like we were aliens on another planet together, or pirates on the same ship in another life. First of all, we're obsessed with theater. Second of all, we're dreamers. We always got marked "Needs To Pay Attention In Class" on our grade school report cards. We both can't wait to blow high school and really study drama, instead of wasting endless boring hours on things like biology.

TigrrEyz took her online name from her favorite book as a kid, Tiger Eyes, by Judy Blume. In the book, the main character's father dies. TigrrEyz's father died when a blood clot formed in his brain. Natalie was only twelve. My parents are divorced, and my dad is not exactly a huge part of my life. So we had that in common, too.

To summarize: we have the perfect relationship. We've shared all this intimate stuff with each other, but we've never had an awkward silence. We've never had a sweaty date. She's never seen me with a zit. I don't have to worry about my hair, or my clothes.

So why would I want to spoil it?

What if TygrrEyz thinks I'm a dork?

"So skip it," Mark told me before breezing out to soccer practice. "Like I keep telling you, online crushes should stay online. IRL, things never work out. Don't risk it."

So maybe he's right. In Real Life, girls with tiger eyes don't go for guys like me. Guys with a basic boring face, not overly cute, not overly ugly, and a body with no particular musculature.

But what does Mark know? He's already got his life mapped out. He's going to be an investment banker. He's going to get engaged when he's twenty-nine, and married when he's thirty. He's even got the block picked out in Boston whcre he's going to live. And you know what? I have no doubt that he will.

He's not a dreamer. He doesn't have romance in his soul. He wouldn't get on the bus to chase down a girl who only exists in bytes and microchips.

But dreamers have to risk, even for just one look. Even if I chickened out and turned right around to hightail it back to school like the complete and utter coward that I am. I had to see her, just once.

So I guess I made my decision. I'm going.